PRAIRIE GOTHIC

EDITED BY
STACEY KONDLA

Prairie Soul Press
www.ThePrairieSoul.com/press

Cover credit:
Maia Kondla Wolf

Something Wicked

… Jim Jackson

Something Wicked this way comes
Like an old grudge you left undone
With you succumb?
When something wick this way comes

Something evil this way flies
On wings of teeth and wing of lies
Are you surprised?
That something evil this way flies

It's the holler on the high prairie
It's the darkness in our hearts
It's the cross you can no longer carry
It's the hate that tears you apart

Something wicked this way comes
With blare of horn and beat of drum
Will you even run?
When something wicked
this way comes

Contents

Introduction
... Stacey Kondla

The prairies are usually ignored or dismissed as flat and boring. But if you live on the prairies, if you've ever taken a walk in the grasslands, if you've stood in a wheat field at night and listened to the coyotes howl, you know the prairies are anything but boring.

I have lived on the prairies all my life and love them with all my heart. The wide open spaces, the big sky, the wind, coulees, cactus, sage, the hum of life and nature on spring days, the green that turns to gold with the heat of summer, the badlands, the foothills, the wildlife that is so quiet and so good at remaining unseen despite the illusion of there being nowhere to hide, the buzz of grasshoppers, the chirp of crickets, the unmistakable cry of a killdeer, the swooping, rocket-fast elegance of a barn swallow, the urban sprawl of prairie cities, the uniqueness and charm of each small town, the goddamn mosquitos that are everywhere–there is so much to celebrate about the prairies! And the prairies at night or in winter are completely separate entities.

As an avid reader, I've noticed that the prairies are often overlooked as a setting for stories, passed over for more exotic or lush locales. And if we look at gothic fiction, those stories are mostly set on the British moors, where gothic fiction originated, or in a worn down mansion on the east coast of the United States, or set on a southern plantation. I have never seen a collection of gothic stories set in the Canadian prairies. So that was part of my motivation to bring an anthology like this to life.

The other reason is, as a child, I had a recurring nightmare. The nightmare always took place on my grandparents' farm. There was a huge white monster that was going to find me and smash me and eat me. I know now the monster in my dreams was inspired by the white monster, the Mugato, that beat the snot out of Captain Kirk in the original *Star Trek* TV series. I loved watching that show with my Dad when I was a child. As an adult, I became intrigued that my mind took that monster and planted it on my grandparents' farm right smack in the middle of the prairies. And that it wanted me. And that I had the same dream over and over.

The nightmare was never graphic, the monster never actually got me, but the psychological fear that it *would* get me was intense. That is why I love gothic fiction so much. Primarily the emotions it can invoke. The heavy weight, the feeling of dread, the casual dismissal that maybe it's all in your head, the terror when you realize you are crazy, or that something actually is going to get you! Oh my god!

That fear paired with setting fascinates me. So, several years ago I started thinking about an anthology of gothic stories set on the Canadian prairies. Then I started talking about it with anthology editors I know and writers in the local writing community. People seemed to enjoy the idea, so when Jim Jackson of Prairie Soul Press expressed interest, I knew we could make this project happen.

The authors we invited to contribute to this anthology are all Canadian prairie authors with diverse backgrounds. They know the prairies, and each one shows unique aspects of prairie life whether the story is set in a city or farm, the past or the present. The stories explore what gothic fiction means to each author and their prairie experience. Incorporating a variety of ghosts, magic, religion, madness, despair, creepy old houses, fear, and monsters–whether they be actual monsters or people that are monsters–the authors all bring a freshness to telling gothic stories. All of the stories have the sophistication found in such stories as *The Yellow Wallpaper* by Charlotte Perkins Gilman or more traditionally gothic stories such as *Frankenstein* by Mary Shelley or *The Picture of Dorian Grey* by Oscar Wilde, blended with the Canadian literary feel of works like *The Painted Door* by Sinclair Ross and an unmistakable contemporary Canadian vibe.

So, as editor of this anthology, I hope you enjoy the twist that the Canadian prairies presents to gothic fiction, and I hope you delight in each of these stories by talented prairie authors as much I have.

Darling House
... PJ Vernon

The house is a monster.

Too looming, too lurching, far too old.

"Happy, my love?" James asks, hoisting a box marked *FRAGILE!* up the porch of the Calgarian craftsman. A century home, narrow and tall and presumably wrought with cash from once-new railroads or once-new oil. I can't find words, so I offer a smile instead. He seems to accept it and makes his way through the front door. Shadow swallows him, and he vanishes.

Our car is parked curbside behind the moving truck, passenger door ajar. I collect a pot packed with framed photos and trace James's steps inside. The inevitability of it all feels cruel.

"I'm worried about you, Amelia," James announces suddenly as I sit across from him in the salon, knitting material on my lap. "We've lived here for months now, and you haven't made a single friend."

"Ellen from knitting group –"

"A *real* friend. How many times have you seen Ellen outside the first Tuesday of the month?"

I remain silent, let his concern sink in, hope he moves past it. But the truth is, I don't desire friends. Not anymore. Not since we've moved here. I've taken to calling the home Darling House. I call it this because it sounds whimsical and plays off the dollhouse dreams I hold secret.

It also blunts the edge of the coldness. The breeze that frosts my neck more and more with the passage of time spent inside endlessly patient Darling House.

"I've got an idea for bunko tomorrow," James tells me. I hate bunko night, but James insists I participate. The women–the frantic hens populating bunko night–are insufferable. Bleached hair and couture blouses too tight for their chardonnay-sculpted frames. Bunko is society's way for society women to carry on day-drinking into the night.

"What idea?" I ask.

"A medium. Richard at the office, his wife Fran is a medium."

"Doesn't sound very Christian. I'm not sure the other ladies –"

"I've already invited her. Through Richard, of course," James smiles. "She's coming over."

Of course.

◊

"I don't like your cellar," Fran says pointedly. She's the last guest. We make our way from the wine glasses and brie and stale crackers abandoned in the dining room and into the foyer.

"What's not to like?"

"There's death down there, Amelia." Interesting Fran doesn't like the cellar on account of death. Death was the talk *du jour* among the women all evening long.

Fran relayed messages from Melissa's late father. Said he no longer blames her for his wife's accident. When Melissa was twelve, she begged her mother to look at a hastily scrawled drawing from the backseat. Mother returned her eyes to the road in time to catch a glimpse of the stop sign she ran. Last thing she saw before the impact snapped her neck.

Fran told Regina she has nothing to worry about. The knotty dollop of blood she flushed down the toilet nine years ago wasn't a miscarriage. Empty silence from the Other Side indicated Regina had never been pregnant. At least, not in that instance.

Suddenly, Melissa and Regina's fermented afternoons make more sense.

"Well, it's an old home," I smile at Fran and open the front door. "I'm sure it's seen quite a bit of death."

"Not like this," Fran whispers. Her eyes–she almost glowers.

I recall the previous owners. The husband, he took a tumble down the front stairs. The upkeep of such an old structure had grown too burdensome for a lonely widow.

"That isn't it, either," Fran says. "The echo, the lingering imprint, is one of violence. And much older. Much, *much* older."

I politely thank her for her company and shut the door.

As I do, I think she's said something else. I think she might've muttered, "He was killing people down there."

I surely misheard.

"Copies of the property records," says James. He's walked in through the front door as the grandfather clock chimed six. Same as every other weeknight without fail. He sets a manila folder on my lap next to my knitting and gently kisses my forehead. "Like you asked for. I'm happy you're occupying your mind with something smart. How's Ellen?"

"She's fine," I tell him. Knitting is all I have now, anyways. No more bunko nights at Darling House. No more bunko nights for me at all. Melissa and Regina have grown cold. But that's okay. I'm cold, too. All the time, I'm cold. All the time, the tips of my fingers tingle with bloodlessness.

I thumb through the copies James made for me. An eclectic mix of owners, renters–Darling House rented for thirteen dollars and twenty-five cents per month in 1914 and this makes me snicker.

As I flip past one record, something calls. I go back to it, read it more carefully.

Frederick Cecire. Candlemaker. Apparently, he built the home, too. Only person to live here till it began collecting renters a decade later.

Candlemaking. I eye my knitting suspiciously. I might try making candles.

"If you'd like to take up a new hobby, please do so where it won't make such a mess," James chastises me, though his smile's still warm. "What happened to knitting? Is all not well with Ellen?"

"Ellen's fine," I whisper, peering out the kitchen windows. "It's too cold outside. It's snowing, and I need flame. The wax is made from animal fat, and it needs to melt down for the mold."

"Take it into the cellar, then," James urges.

I recall Fran's words. Fran doesn't like our cellar. *He's killing people down there.*

I collect my things, bringing the spools of wick, my blocks of fatty wax, my scissors, into my arms, and make for the cellar.

"Good girl, Amelia," James calls lovingly from behind.

Taking the groaning stairs one slow step at a time, I enter the moist space. Down here, standing on uneven concrete below pine rafters so ancient they've petrified, I understand why Fran doesn't like the cellar. Down here, I grow even colder.

◇

It's my first trip outside Darling House in almost two months. Ellen says I've become a shut-in, and I'm much too young for that sort of behavior. James now seems to secretly enjoy that I stay in the home. No sense becoming overwhelmed outside, he muses pleasantly.

The glass door trips a bell wire, calling the antique shop's clerk over. As he greets me, I hoist the object I've been carrying onto his desk. The object I'd spotted beneath a cobwebbed pile of junk in a dark corner of Darling House's cellar.

"I was wondering if you might have candles from a mold like this one?" I ask. The clerk eyes the candle mold, the elegant *C.C.* stamped into one side.

"Cecire Candles." He sucks air through the gap in his front teeth. "Famous throughout the prairies in his day. Frederick lived in Calgary, you know."

"I know."

He rests his chin in the groove between his thumb and forefinger. "Come with me."

I follow him to a dining table for sale in a back nook. It's flanked by an ornate hutch–slick cherry wood or something like it. The table settings are silver and exquisite. A swirling candelabra rests in the very center and holds ten candles, long and thin and pointy. Their color, red with a warmth that's almost too deep.

"Those are Cecire candles, ma'am." A proud nod. "His signature color."

"I'll take them," I say. "And the candelabra."

"What a beautiful piece," James notes, setting his crocodile briefcase on the dining room table. Six o'clock, sharp. "Really, it's quite lovely."

"The candles, they're Cecire candles. Their maker, Frederick, built this house."

James takes my hand, kisses the back of it, "You're a precocious little historian, aren't you, my love?"

"I'd like to have dinner in here this evening," I tell James. He grins in agreement.

I strike a kitchen match against its box and sulfur tickles my nose. As I light the final candle, arms wrap around my waist, and I flinch.

"The meat looks fabulous," James whispers in my ear. Both his hands travel down to my hips, then beneath the waistline of my slacks. I step sideways and away from his eager fingers.

"Have a seat." I refill his wine from a glass decanter and take my own chair across the table. As he cuts into the roast with a freshly sharpened boning knife–a precise medium-rare–droplets of red gather and grow from the center, roll down cooked flesh as bloody teardrops, and strike the bone china plate below.

My eyes dart to the candles. At the wicks, just below their dancing flames, the wax does the same. In almost exactly the same way.

In the cellar, I run my palm against the exposed river stone foundation. Cold. The same temperature as my hand atop it. My fingers stop every so often at tiny flecks stuck to the walls. Black flecks long since hardened the way sap turns to amber. Black, but whispers of red remain. Red like the Cecire candles upstairs.

And at last, I know. I know what Fran doesn't like. I know what Frederick Cecire has done.

◊

The grandfather clock strikes six. One lyrical chime for each hour since noon. I set my knitting on my lap, clench my aching hands. Hard work making candles, and I've left far more than a proper mess in the cellar. Dull pain radiates from my shoulders. All my muscles are tense and riddled with knots.

My eyes find the front door, visible from my leather high-back in the salon. I wait for James's return from the office. I wait for James to ask me how Ellen's doing. To congratulate me on a day well spent at home. Alone.

But the door stays shut.

Then my eyes meander to the entryway table. To the new silver candlestick holder resting there, and the new red candle it grips. The flame paints the wall in dancing shadow. Wax, crimson and clotted, drips down its sleek shape.

For a moment, I consider inviting Fran back to Darling House.

I wonder what she might have to say now.

Dry Town

... Sarah L. Johnson

Cardston. The town time ran away from. Where women still wear house dresses, four kids is a good start, and a man working nine-to-five can support every one of them as they skip past the white granite Temple singing some cultish kiddie hymn about families being together forever. Then there's retiree migrants that hit sixty and head to Mecca. Vivacious empty nesters, on their arrival too young to be cast in a Viagra commercial, now she wears housedresses and his pants have an elastic waist. Nothing'll age you three decades overnight like a Southern Alberta dry town.

Not just Mormons, of course. Snuggled up to rez land, there's loads of Indians, farm folk, and a healthy Filipino population on account of all the olds needing care. Only thing you won't find is people like me. Something about Cardston creates a queer vacuum that defies statistical probability. But if one did exist, they'd be tolerated, because they run the only place you can get a decent drink around here.

"Bad luck," I say, scrubbing the sweat from my eyes and staring up at the shattered Red Rooster sign. Omens don't get much clearer. I've lived every day of my twenty-eight years in this backwater, and Lord willing, this will be my last. I kick what appears to be the culprit, a baseball, down a gutter that hasn't seen a drop of wet in almost three months. The Red Rooster is my place. The sign, a cracked and faded disaster, happens to be the original from the old convenience store chain. A steel-framed, glass-box relic. No one ever took it away, and it never stopped working, so I never bothered to change it.

Someone winged a ball through my sign last night, but it's no hate crime. Mormon kids shoot hoops like no one's business, but they are the world's shittiest baseball players. True story. I glance across the street beyond the town's sad monument to fame, the Fay Wray Fountain, to the ball diamond. Fence glinting in the morning sun, red shale, surrounded by a drought scorched field. End of an era, I guess. No fixing a baseball right through the rooster. I'm moving on anyway.

Ghostly odors of Coke syrup and Twizzlers waft out as I open the front door and make my way through the gloom. Not fancy, but it's got a bar, stools, and a few tables that don't wobble too bad if you shim them with coasters. I've even got a little kitchen in the back. On paper, it's a coffee shop, which in Mormonville is as likely to thrive as a gay bar. I flick on the lights, unwrap a Jolly Rancher, and pop it into my mouth. Grape. More bad luck. In the kitchen, I pull the aluminum trays of funeral potatoes and sliced ham out of the fridge and slide them in the ovens. Then I empty the dishwasher, grab two big bags of ice, and head out front to fill the tubs.

"Mornin', Dusty Spencer."

"Flippin-jeez, Marveen!" I nearly choke on my perfectly chokable Jolly Rancher. "What the hell?"

She glances up, silver waves falling loose over her shoulders. No Cardston short-curl for her. She studies the cards fanned out on the bar in front of her. "Got nowhere else to be."

"Are you…" I shouldn't even engage. "Have you been here the whole time?"

Dozens of bracelets chime on her skinny wrists as she flips the cards over. "Hmm, Frog Full of Marbles. Looks like you've taken some damage, and the Midnight Plumber suggests you might take more."

"That's not a real tarot deck."

"Don't matter," she says, flipping one last card, placing it in the center, tapping it with her gnarled wand of an index finger. "Spear of Light."

"Very funny, Marv."

"Rain gon' come, kid. Soon."

"Yeah, well I've got a crowd of people coming. Sooner."

"That's why you're up and at 'em so early." Marveen grins, revealing gold bicuspids. "Always loved a funeral."

"Please don't joke about this."

"I'm old and allowed to joke about anything I want, Dusty." She cuts the deck and pulls out another card. "And the Duchess of Duty-Free Smokes agrees with me."

Outside, the wind kicks up and shards of shattered rooster tail rattle like a snare drum. I'm going to have to get up there with some tape before the crowd arrives.

Christ, it's another cooker out there. The a/c is already struggling to keep ahead of the heat, and the ovens aren't helping.

I fill a shot glass and slide it across the bar.

"Scotch?" she asks.

I nod.

"Now who's joking?"

"Best I got, and the least I can do. On the house."

She claws the shot closer. "Join me?"

"Auction closes in six hours. Then I'll join you."

Marveen downs the whiskey in one, cackling low in her throat as she swallows. I wish I could get rid of her. At the same time, I'm glad she's here.

"I'm doing what I can," I say. "Opening the place early, feeding a hundred grief-stricken Mormons I don't actually have space for."

"Respect for the dead, aren't you a peach."

I pluck out my phone and check the private auction room bids. Collectors swarm like sharks around a bleeding tuna. Marveen always said I ought to get out of here, and once the money is deposited with my skeezebag broker, I'm gone. You'd think she'd be happy.

"What're you feeding the wailing mob, anyway?" she asks.

"A legion's worth of ham, and hash brown casserole. Think that'll do?"

Marveen pushes her empty glass at me. "Church punch?"

"Pineapple, cranberry, and ginger ale on ice."

"Ambrosia?"

"Relief Society ladies are on that." I tuck the phone in my back pocket and pour her another. "Jell-O salad recipes are a Temple endowment, and apparently I'm not worthy."

"Dried-up cunts, the all of 'em." She lazily shuffles her deck. "Y'know, I would have given it to you, had you asked."

She's not talking about Jell-O, and the sweat on my skin ices over. "Well shit, Marv. My bad. Let me hop in my time machine."

She bangs back the whiskey and pulls a face. "Best you got, my ass. Where you hidin' the good stuff anyway?"

"Someplace no one would ever care to look," I say, grabbing a roll of duct tape. "I'm going out to fix the sign."

August sun hammers me the second I set foot outside under a sky clear blue as a bottle of Bombay Sapphire. It last rained in May and not a drop since, though it came close a few days ago. Wind whipping down the wide boulevard of Temple Street. Clouds cumulating. Every blade of grass quivering in the electric air. A single bolt of lightning and a clap of thunder so loud you'd swear it came from the hands of God. And nothing. Three months of relentless arid heat. Three months never seeing the mercury dip below twenty-eight degrees even in the dark hours before dawn.

Lightning, but no rain. This town is burning.

I'm not about to burn with it. I check my phone, watching bids tick up as the clock ticks down. The ladder clanks as I haul it from the storage shed and extend it against the crumbling stucco of the Red Rooster. Last time I was up here was the night it nearly rained, and I thought I was going to be electrocuted. Tape slung over my wrist, I start climbing.

"Morning, Brother Spencer," a Utah accent calls from the ground. "Where've you been keeping?"

I drop my forehead against an aluminum rung. "Here, which is the last place you'd ever look, Elder Tran."

"Haven't seen you in church lately."

"Because I haven't gone. Where's your companion?"

"Elder Raymond'll be along. I slipped out of the service early."

"Assigned missionary companions aren't supposed to let each other out of their sight, as I understand it."

"I required urgent use of the facilities."

"Bit different than sneaking into the baptismal font for a quick fuck during Sacrament Meeting."

"Jeez, Dusty. I don't think the dead heard you."

I shiver as the sun sears the back of my neck. "They heard me just fine. What do you want, Elder Tran?"

He steps up to steady the ladder. "To be of service, Brother Spencer. You've got a chapel full of folks hungry the way only death can make 'em headed over in a few minutes. What happened to your sign?"

I consider the shattered rooster tail, slide to the ground, and turn around to face the beautiful Vietnamese kid from St. George, Utah. "Nothing that can't wait."

"Roasting like a ding-dang duck out here," he says, squinting at the sizzling sky. "Thought sure we were gonna get rain the other night. I just can't believe what happened. And I can't believe you didn't come to the service."

"Like you said, I got a job to do." A gust of hot wind shakes the ladder but cools nothing. Only job prairie wind has is to desiccate everything in its path, sucking whatever moisture remains out of burnt beige lawns and burnt beige people. A drop of sweat slides from Elder Tran's side part, down his temple, and it's all I can do not to catch it with my tongue. "Help me set out the food?"

Marveen doesn't look up when we duck into the comparatively cool bar that smells of ham, and potatoes bubbling brown with cheese, and canned mushroom soup. She doesn't look, though I see she's got the bottle in front of her. I won't make an issue of it. She can hold her liquor, drink any man under the table and then some. Hopefully she'll just sit, flip her cards, help herself to my Balvenie, and keep quiet.

Elder Tran looks uncomfortable, but I don't think it's Marveen; he doesn't notice her as his shiny shoes slide over the dingy tiles. "Never been in here before."

"You don't have to stay."

He takes my hand, pulling me close enough to smell sweat mingled with Right Guard leaking through regulation short-sleeve. "I know you're hurting, Dusty. But she's with our Heavenly Father now. You'll see her again."

"Would you stop with that shit?" I close the distance between us. "You're the weirdest missionary I ever met."

He places a hand over his heart. "The Lord and me are solid. No secrets between us, and the way I see it, His judgment is all that matters."

"That's what I'm worried about."

"You smell like candy," he says and the moment my lips brush his, the front door jingles and he leaps out of my arms.

"Not even noon and the corn is popping off the cob!" a deep voice booms. "Morning, Dusty... Elder Tran, where's your companion?"

"Here, Bishop." A chubby freckle-faced kid pushes through the door carrying three enormous Tupperware containers, followed by the Relief Society president holding a horrible floral arrangement matching her horrible dress.

"Goodness, thank you, Elder Raymond," she says, pretty mouth pouting. "I've run my nylons. So hot I'm this close to taking them off!"

Marveen grunts and I give her a look. Am I warning or pleading? All I know is every complicated relationship I have in this town is walking through my front door.

"Lemme help with that, Sister Schaeffer." Elder Tran dashes over and takes the flowers. I dig out a bottle of clear nail polish from behind the bar and she accepts it gratefully, hiking her skirt up to the edge of her garments to paint over the snag in her pantyhose.

"Good day for a cold one," Bishop Layton says, pausing for a reaction only he would feel entitled to, and then chortles like the sweating redneck he is under that wretched tie. "Jokes. Though we all know Sister

Manybears was no stranger to the Rooster. Mighty good of you, Dusty. Hosting her funeral lunch." The big man I've known most of my life, who has never once *not* reminded me of a bag of mayonnaise, gives me a once-over in my Blockbuster T-shirt and jeans. "Missed you at the service."

"Service is coming to me, Bishop."

"More'n you know," Marveen mutters and tugs the stopper off the Scotch bottle with her teeth.

"Jesus," I whisper.

"Beg pardon?" the Bishop asks.

"Gotta get food out of the oven, 'scuse me."

Elder Tran trips along after me. We get the ham and potatoes set out on folding tables soon whimpering under the weight of a feast. The Relief Society sisters bustle in with rolls, squares, salads, and Jell-O with wonders suspended inside: carrots, raisins, imitation crab, and who knows what else.

General population trickles in next. Retirees and lifers. House dresses, control-top nylons, more bad ties, and mail-order suits. Layers of piety. They must be broiling in their magic ginch. Weirdest of all, there's kids running around the Red Rooster for the first time in twenty years. Ghoulishly kitted out in their memento mori Sunday best. Marveen observes with great interest when a couple of them sneak around behind the bar, hiding from their friends in an impromptu game of hide-and-seek.

"Here comes the ambrosia." Elder Tran squeezes my arm and zips back to Elder Raymond's side as the Bishop's much younger wife, and my best friend in the world, claps an enormous bowl of fluffy marshmallow Jell-O heaven onto the table.

"Where were you?" she demands, dark eyes wet in their bruised hollows.

"Not really a funeral person, Ada. You know that."

"Gosh, I'm sorry. I didn't realize this was about you."

"Is the Mayonnaise Man not a big enough shoulder to cry on?"

"Be respectful. He's the Bishop, and a dentist."

"He's a prick and I can't believe you married him."

I expect her to slug me, but instead those eyes spill over. "Dusty... my mom is gone."

She falls into my arms, and I know in that moment that the outer darkness is too good for me. I'm worse than a bad friend. Worse than her eggy dentist dad-husband, playing his Bishop role to the hilt in my bar. Worse than every hypocrite in this town who furtively runs out for milk and bread, desperate for liquid escape from seven kids and Family Home Evening.

Marveen covers her ears and drops her head onto the bar. I don't blame her. I've seen Ada cry maybe twice in our lives. It's a big deal. It hurts.

"Ada," I whisper into her silky black hair. "I'm so goddamn sorry."

She wipes her wet face on my shoulder and pulls back. "It's the weirdest thing. I was happy that night, waiting for the rain. Giddy almost. The air felt... swollen, like a living thing about to burst. I thought about coming here, so the three of us could watch the downpour together like we used to."

She's waiting for me to commiserate, share my own happy memories. But my throat is blocked with a lump the size of the baseball that shattered my sign. My mom died when I was twelve, and somehow I found another. How lucky is that? Except now she's dead too.

"Who gets struck by lightning?" Ada says. "What was she doing in the middle of the ball diamond, and with her gun?"

I shrug, unwrapping another Jolly Rancher. Fucking grape, again. Through the window, I make out the blackened patch of earth on the edge of the ball diamond. I shouldn't laugh, but I can't help it. "I guess…I mean, now it's hard to imagine her dying any other way, you know?"

"You've got a point." Ada laughs with me and I've never loved her more, the daughter of the woman who saved me. My family, in every way that matters. She pulls a tattered tissue out of her skirt pocket and dabs her forehead. "Lord, it's flippin' hot. Between crying and sweating, I'm turning into an old corn husk. I need a drink. A real one. Not this church punch bullshit."

"On it." I dart behind the bar, shooing the kids away.

Marveen turns over a card that looks like a beach ball carrying a briefcase. "Ah, the Banker. He's a lucky one."

"I don't need luck. Auction closes in a few hours," I say, perusing my selection for something that would please the Bishop's wife.

Marveen slides the Balvenie towards me. "Gal's got her mother's fine taste. Wasted in a town like this. On a man like that."

Bishop Layton's repulsive chortle thunders across the bar as if on cue.

When I return with solo cups of "punch" I find Ada chatting with Elder Raymond and Elder Tran. She croons and strokes them like the earnest puppies they are. And they are her pets. They have dinner at the Bishop's house practically every night, which means the Bishop's wife gets to cook a full-trimmings meal every night of her life. How lucky can a girl get?

I push a cup into her hand and she gulps it in one.

"Hope you're not pregnant or anything," I say and Elder Tran's eyes bulge.

"Why would I have a baby?" She ruffles his hair. "I've got these two precious poodles, so young and far from home. Mama said there's enough kids out there needing mothers without going and making more."

Elder Raymond responds with an adoring grin. "Children are a blessing, Sister."

"And parents are the curse. They die and leave you all alone, with what apparently is the best you can do in this town." She eyes Bishop Layton over the rim of her glass. "Another, if you please, Dusty."

I get Ada another drink, then bus tables, fill the water jugs, and accept condolences, while she makes her rounds, fulfilling her obligation as bereft daughter and pillar of the community. As we shoulder our way through the humid crowd, Marveen watches us like a mother bear but doesn't speak to a soul.

Back in the kitchen, I find Elder Tran loading plates into the dishwasher. He blots his forehead with a towel. "Cheese 'n' rice it's a sauna in here."

"Thanks for being of service." I kiss the back of his damp neck, loving the way he quivers.

The door bangs and Ada swans in, floral skirt sailing behind her, blouse open one button too many for a dry town. Sweat glimmers on her sternum and a smile slants across her face. "Why, Elder Tran, where's your companion?"

Elder Tran flips the towel over his shoulder. "Had to use the facilities, Sister."

She slips her arm around my waist and stands on tip-toe, whiskey-wet mouth at my ear. "I know."

I nod to Elder Tran. "I'll be back in a minute."

Taking Ada's hand, I tow her out of the kitchen and over to the bar where she slides onto the stool next to Marveen, who doesn't speak but seems pleased for the company nevertheless.

"Okay." I brace my hands on the bar because I can't feel my legs. "What do you mean, you know?"

"Lord, don't look so scared. I'd never say anything."

"About?"

She reaches over, wrapping her hands around my wrists. "Elder Tran, dummy. I know what you two have been up to in the baptismal font."

"Y'do?"

She shrugs. "Who do you think leaves it unlocked for you?"

I exhale, blood rushing back into my heart. "Another for my wingman?"

I pour a healthy slug into her cup, which we share. I pour another. We trade the cup back and forth, accompanied by the sound of Marveen shuffling her cards.

Finally Ada sighs, taking my hand, rubbing her thumb over my skin like she used to when we were kids and I'd sneak into her room to sleep on her floor. Reaching down from her bed when I'd wake up from a bad dream.

"I'm staying at her place tonight," she says, eyes glassy with liquor and tears. "Stay with me?"

Under the social din, the wind wrenches my wrecked sign. I think of the phone in my pocket, and the minutes slipping away. I promised myself that as soon as that alarm rang, no matter what I was doing or in the middle of, no matter what, I was leaving. For good.

"We can start going through her stuff tomorrow. You're welcome to anything you want."

"I dunno, Ada…"

"Not even her whiskey collection?"

"Huh?" I say, hoping it sounds authentic.

"You didn't know?" she asks. "She and my aunties went looting abandoned estates right before the Oldman dam flooded them. Some of those bottles are worth a lot. She'd want you to have something."

I'm legless once again, not because I'm touched, though I am, or because I'm surprised, because I'm not. Of course I knew about her collection of pilfered liquor. She told me the stories herself.

Marveen crows and waves a card around. "The Land Pirate! Lord, I went on some raids in my day. Shoulda seen the treasure those rich white folks left behind."

It dawns on me that I have an opportunity. When I was a kid, my worst dreams, my worst fears, were of being sent away. Nothing can undo what I did, but maybe God is giving me a chance. A way to stay.

Bishop Layton undulates to the bar and rests one immaculate dentist's hand on Ada's shoulder. "Bout ready to skedaddle, dear?"

She shrugs him off. "Me and Dusty are staying at Mom's tonight, start sorting through all her junk."

Bishop Layton recovers from a near-frown and chuckles, giving me the side eye. "No offense, Brother Spencer, but don't you think that's best left to family?"

"Dusty is the only family I have left, *dear*. 'Scuse me, there's a few I didn't get to say hello to." She pushes the red cup across the bar into my hand. "Think about it, okay?"

She glides off, no trace of a slur in her step or her speech.

"Always could hold her liquor," Marveen says with a hint of something like pride.

The mayonnaisian blinks at me, bewildered.

"Bishop." I lift the solo cup to my lips and knock it back.

He wanders off dazed, as though he's been struck by lightning. I take a breath, remind myself I'm not a hateful person. I remind myself of the time he opened his clinic at 2 a.m. when fifteen–year–old me fell out of Ada's window. Those immaculate hands were gentle as he extracted my eyetooth from my tongue. Afterward, one of those hands patted Ada's cheek, assuring her I'd be fine. She was also fifteen. The wind buffets the windows and I pull out my phone. Three more hours to decide.

"Spear of Light," Marveen says, tapping the crude sketch of a warrior–ish woman holding a gleaming polearm. "That's twice now."

Suddenly I'm exhausted and I lean my full weight onto the bar. "Why won't you leave? I said I was sorry."

I jump back as Marveen's deck explodes from her hands and I'm pelted with fake tarot cards.

"Your apologies ain't worth a crooked ear of corn, you little shit. You owe me."

"I'm trying my best to make it right."

"And you gonna. I can't judge you too hard, doing what you did. How's I got it in the first place wasn't any more noble. But now you gonna do what you should have done years ago. And you gonna take her with you."

Wind batters the windows again and the daylight abruptly dims.

"Storm's coming in!" Elder Tran shouts, dashing to the front window.

"Told you," Marveen says, black eyes brimming with grief, exactly like her daughter's. "Rain gon' come."

A metallic screech ripples through the startled congregation.

"Shit, the sign." I leap over the bar. Halfway to the door, I turn back and tug Ada aside. "I can't stay, Ada. Not another night in this town. And you can't either."

"What? Why? What's going on?"

I breathe deep, knowing what I'm committing to, what I'll eventually have to explain. "I'm leaving, right now. Come with me."

She laughs, hiccups, and goes silent. "Wait, serious?"

"It's what your mom wants, what she always wanted. For us to get out of here."

Her eyes flick to her husband, goggling with the rest of them at the heavy indigo clouds blotting out the sun. Then she's searching my face. Searching my soul.

She squeezes my hand, thumb stroking. "Go fix your sign."

The storm roils overhead as I muscle the door open and step outside, hugging the walls of the building. The wind nearly rips the ladder out of my hands as I haul it out of the shed and lean it against the stucco.

Bad luck, that's all. She wasn't supposed to be home. The Lethbridge broker, skeezebag though he was, assured me this was my ticket out. No one was supposed to know. I even wore a ski mask in case someone saw (as Marveen told me herself, there's an art to this deplorable practice). No one would know it was Dusty Spencer. Marveen Manybears didn't know it was her wayward foster kid.

Chasing a burglar across the baseball field with her shotgun as the sky rumbled.

Lightning, but no rain.

The sign sways and squeals in the wind. I climb the rungs carefully and crawl onto the roof. The storm churns as I reach into the sign, right through the hole in the Red Rooster. My phone trumpets with the special alert, meaning someone clicked the exorbitant "buy now" bid. The auction is closed, and Ada and I are getting out of here.

My hands wrap around the duct-taped box containing a bottle of Macallan 1926 Fine & Rare, just as I feel the first drops of rain on the back of my neck. And every hair on my body stands on end.

Mini McDonagh Manor

... Mike Thorn

The two-foot tall, miniature house on Julie's cluttered desktop was a nearly identical, downsized replica of her childhood home–a distinct heritage manor located in Bergen, Alberta. It was a house of pain and a house of secrets, but also a house filled with the kinds of precious, painfully delicate memories that emerge only before adulthood takes hold. And she, Julie McDonagh, had just fashioned it herself.

She rubbed at her sleep-crusty eyes and said, "Well, goddamn."

When Julie had first got word of her mother's death, her department manager at Kabocha Design had offered her a professionally chaste hand on the shoulder and two days of bereavement leave. To get things in order, two days was all Julie had needed. Motivated to drag herself from the swampy undercurrents of mourning and even more motivated to create something, she'd spent every moment of paid grief conducting online research, finding the right materials for the project at hand.

Then came the building process, which Julie could remember no more clearly than the narrative of any cryptic dream from years past. She couldn't exactly say *why* she'd decided to make the thing–it had simply happened.

And now, right here, in reconstructed tabletop form, was the house where her mother had died. As for the proverbial and not-so-proverbial skeletons: those had gone out with Natalie McDonagh, and Julie had no intention of bringing them back to life.

Not now, not ever.

Beside the mini heritage home–all worn wood and tiny aged shingles and brickwork–Julie's Android buzzed a loud reminder. Its screen flashed, *Don't forget to bring your thumb drive for the meeting.*

For the first time since she'd gotten the call from her estranged brother Bill, she wept.

Todd made a show of rolling his muscular shoulders as he pulled his undershirt on over his head. He gave Julie a toothy smile that suggested the sex had been much better for him than for her. He ran a hand through his thinning black hair and wiggled his substantial eyebrows. "You know," he said, "it really wouldn't be a problem for me to stick around for some tomorrow-morning delight. Two for the price of one?"

Julie pulled the covers over her breasts and shook her head. "No, I need some time alone. I'm still processing."

She was using her grief as an excuse, and it made her feel a little guilty, but only for a moment. She barely knew this guy, and she could already tell their Tinder-orchestrated arrangement wouldn't be a long-term thing.

Todd was a distraction, and generally he seemed to understand this without objection.

Slipping back into his briefs, Todd looked up at the Patti Smith poster hanging over Julie's bed. "Who's that chick?" he asked.

"Patti Smith," Julie replied tonelessly. "That's a rare poster replica of her best album, *Radio Ethiopia*."

Todd paused, as if processing this information. Julie knew he would forget about it by the time he left the room. With an awkward smile, he nodded toward the replica on the desk. "That thing creeps me the fuck out, I've gotta say. When we were going at it, I caught it out the corner of my eye and thought something might fly through its little door and possess my naked body."

Tactless, but not cruel. Typical Todd.

Julie pinched the bridge of her nose and squeezed her eyes shut. This was the first time they'd hooked up at her place, and she'd ensured that everything had occurred in darkness. Now that Todd was drawing attention to Mini McDonagh Manor, she felt more naked than she had during sex.

"Hey, I'm sorry," Todd said. "I didn't mean to hurt your feelings."

Too tired to get into it, Julie replied, "I just need to get some sleep."

Todd zipped up his jeans and nodded. He didn't say anything to lighten the mood. He didn't stoop down to kiss her before he left. He turned around, and shutting the door behind himself, made his message loud and clear.

As Julie heard his engine revving on the driveway, she murmured, "Good riddance."

In her periphery, she saw something flicker behind the front window of Mini McDonagh. Quick and fluttery, like a moth flitting against a lightbulb.

You saw nothing, she thought. *You're stressed and sleep-deprived and sexually unsatisfied.* She repeated the thought until she almost believed it, then slipped into the sleep she'd been craving.

She dreamed that her mother crawled under the sheets beside her, held her close, and whispered something in her ear. Muddled by the irrational language of dreams, Natalie McDonagh's words were unintelligible. But when Julie awoke, she swore she still felt the weight and warmth of another body under the blankets. And she knew that whoever she'd felt in her dream was not her mother, but someone (or something) else in disguise.

A mourning nightmare. That's all it was. Her self-talk almost convinced her it was the truth.

Almost.

She pulled the sheets tighter and rolled onto her back, turning to face the miniature heritage home. Nothing moved inside, but there was something different about it. It took her a second to pinpoint what it was.

The miniature top floor loft window had been busted open. The hole in its center, smaller than a cherry tomato, was too proportionally precise to be ignored–of course, the *real* hole was much bigger, the hole those vigilante bastards had left in the wake of her father's suspicious death. Julie remembered looking down at the stone lying on the loft carpet, surrounded by glittering shards of glass, and weeping so hard it made her chest hurt.

"Why, Mommy?" she'd asked, over and over and over. "Why would they do that?"

Get up. The thought was loud and instantaneous, as if broadcast from elsewhere. Quivering, Julie fumbled into a shirt and underwear, snatched her cellphone from the bedside table, and exited the room to make a call. Her manager sounded obligatorily empathetic when she told him she wasn't feeling well, and that she would need to stay home for the day. What he didn't know was that she was also planning to make the same call for the next two days.

She hadn't revisited McDonagh Manor the entire time she'd been in Bergen for the funeral. Now, overriding all her mental interventions of logic and reason, she committed to a single, definite goal: she would drive there today, and she would finally put to rest what years of therapy and avoidance had never resolved.

How? She didn't know. She only knew it needed to be done.

Her mind raised the image of the miniature house on her desktop, broken window in high definition. "Don't try to scare me," she said aloud.

She considered bursting back into her room to destroy the thing, wielding it over her head and slamming it down on the hardwood floor. She stood in the hallway, shoulders bunched up as if she was bracing for combat. *No, the miniature is not the thing. The* house *is the thing.* Still posing like a boxer about to enter the ring, she pondered the idea of showering, but ditched it after a second of consideration. She returned to her room and averted her gaze from Mini McDonagh Manor as she got into jeans and a sweater.

"Enough's enough," she said.

A woman could only take so much pain before she took matters into her own hands.

The Toyota's winter tires performed dutifully as Julie cruised the snow-padded highway, her speakers blasting Patti Smith. In her periphery, round hay bales flicked by in a monotonous procession. She stared ahead at the rolling passage of whiteness, trying to formulate something like a plan. This was pure compulsion, something like the feeling that had driven her to reconstruct her childhood home in miniature.

But when she got there... what? Would she see if Bill was around? Or would she go straight to the heritage home to look at its aging face one final time?

She remembered Daddy's cold wrist, slippery with sweat, and the whisper of his tank top against the hardwood. She remembered her mother's robotic tone as she repeated, "The cellar, Julie, the cellar. The cellar. The cellar. The cellar."

And she remembered that, in the dimmest slivers of moonlight creeping through the curtain, she'd seen a wet trail snaking behind Daddy's busted head. It had taken a long time to clean that up, but Julie hadn't been around to help with that part.

That had been up to Mom.

Even despite the power and volume of Patti Smith's voice, Julie recalled the thumps and cracks that always used to signify Dad had come home and was making his power known. The steering wheel, still taking its time to warm, felt something like a dead man's bones in her grip.

"What," Bill said, a statement rather than a question, as soon as Julie stepped onto the sidewalk outside his house. He sat on his front porch, a massive Tim Hortons coffee in one hand and a cigarette smoldering in the other. Snow piled on his oversized toque, his eyes unblinking from a face blotched by age and disregard.

Julie shrugged, feeling ludicrous inside her unzipped parka. "I'm not allowed to come visit my brother?"

"On a workday. After decades of not seeing me." Bill's chapped lips quivered. His vein-webbed nose was red. "What gives?"

That's right. It is *a workday. So, what's he doing at home?* Julie dismissed the mental question; he was here, and that was what mattered.

"How've you been since the funeral?" she asked.

"Fucking terrible, same as always." Bill slurped coffee and chased it with a drag from his smoke. "Geena's trying to take the kids away from me, work's hard, and my foreman's a fucking asshole."

A snowflake landed on the tip of Julie's nose, a tiny cold reminder that winter had no intentions of leaving anytime soon. She wiped it away with her sleeve. "Can I come sit with you for a minute?"

"Why," Bill grunted.

"Just to talk for a minute? Can't we do that? Talk?"

Bill flicked away his cig butt and stood up. "Nothing to talk about."

As he turned to reenter his house, Julie finally voiced what had been stirring in her subconscious ever since she'd built the mini manor. "Something's pretending to be our dead mother, and I think it's the same thing that took a hold of Dad."

Bill paused with the doorknob in his hand. "You fucked me up for a long time, Julie." He turned back to face her. "I'm only gonna say one thing, and then we're through. Here's the fucking truth: all your talk of *the thing* that got hold of Pop, that shit broke my brain. You went off and lived your life while I was stuck here in middle of nowhere Hellberta. I did everything I could to forget–therapy, meds, you name it. Got myself to a place where I could accept things as they are. You and me both know the truth. He was a shitty, abusive dad–end of story. Nothing else to it. You can't just come back here and bring that stuff back. No way."

Julie took a step closer to the porch. "Yeah, we do both know the truth. And that's not it. Look, I'm sorry you've had to deal with all this pain, but it hasn't been easy for me either, Billy."

"Oh, fuck that. Don't make this about you."

"I helped Mom move the body," Julie said, and the words sounded brutally loud. It was only now that she really felt the winter silence. Somewhere in the distance, tires hissed through slush. Muffled by the snow, a dog barked. "And when I was walking up the stairs," she continued, "I saw it slipping out through the living room. It was tall, and it looked strong as hell, walking upright through the house. I can't even attempt to describe it, Bill. It was like the worst vision you could ever have on the strongest psychedelic you could ever take–you've done them all; you know what I'm saying." Her mind resurrected the image of something humanoid, blurry around the edges, as if it was in the process of taking full form. The thing had looked like it was sucking the shadows out of the room. Although she'd seen no features on its non-face, she had *felt* its vitality and awareness. She gulped. "I knew it sensed me watching, but it didn't care. It just got up and left... And it wasn't a relief, because I always knew it would come back. Somehow I knew that."

Bill fumbled his cigarettes back out of his jacket and jammed another one between his lips. "Fuck it. I've got a few minutes, and I mean a *few*. Then I've gotta pick up the kids."

Julie cocooned the mug of Folgers coffee between her palms, making real eye contact with her brother for the first time in nearly thirty years.

They sat at his small kitchen table, the air blue and warm with cigarette smoke. Behind Bill, dishes cluttered ancient laminate counters, wafting aromas of week-old canned spaghetti and stale animal fat. He stubbed his third cigarette into an ashtray, leaning back and wearing an expression Julie had seen too many times. The eyes staring out of his lined and hairy face were the same eyes that used to stare pleadingly at her in the darkness of their childhood home, imploring her for answers or protection as the unfeeling sounds of domestic violence corroded their shared innocence.

Julie had told him about the miniature manor, how the hole had appeared in its front window, and she'd relayed the vivid dream of her not-mother joining her in bed. Surprising herself, she now removed one hand from the warm mug and touched his fingers.

"It always pretends to be someone you love, someone you know. That's how it gets in. I've only seen it once, the night I helped Mom move the body... but it didn't die with Dad. As soon as he was got rid of, it looked for another –"

"Host." Bill shifted his haunted gaze. "Like a fucking parasite."

"Yeah," Julie said. "And I think I resurrected it. I think it channeled through me somehow... I didn't feel like I had any control. It was like I was in a fugue state or something. I think I might have brought it back as, I don't know, some evil embryo or something, inside the house I built."

Staring into a vanishing whorl of smoke, Bill said, "I always thought it might have been hiding inside those men who busted our window. Remember how scared we were? I knew Mom had done something to get rid of Dad, no matter how much she stuck to her alibi–*Daddy had to go away on a trip. He's not coming back.* But I was in the loft when that shit went down... I saw those trucks pull up, like a fucking battalion, and I heard all those men screaming and yelling. *You murdering bitch! Come get some!* Somehow they launched a rock the size of a watermelon through that window, and I don't know what made me do it, but I stepped around all the glass on the carpet to get a look at them. I was scared shitless, but I looked down and saw this one guy–I think he ran the corner store. A wiry fucker named Herman or Howard or something. He was smiling, Julie. He looked as happy as a man watching his daughter take her vows."

Without missing a beat, Julie said, "Let's torch it. Let's go there in the middle of the night and burn that house to the ground."

Bill released his hand from her grip and hacked into his fist. "You kidding me? That thing was in the will for me and I need the goddamn money."

"Don't you want to get rid of the memories? Don't you want to be free of this thing?"

Bill laughed in disbelief and raised his hands. "Whoa, hold up. I'm already trying my best to be free. You're the one who decided to come along and fuck that up for me. I mean, what the hell were you thinking, driving all the way back here? You thought you could just drag back these old superstitions and convince me to burn away a million bucks' worth of property? Sorry if you're jealous, sis, but that house is *mine*."

Julie saw pure conviction in her brother's wide, scarlet-circled eyes. She looked down at the crumb-littered tabletop and thought, *What the hell* were *you thinking? You really believe it would make sense to burn*

the house down? What good would that do? So she'd
sensed something in her bedroom–as real as it had been
to her, why should she expect Bill to chalk it up to
anything more than a grief-induced hallucination?

She turned her head toward the door and spoke in a
near-whisper, "Okay, I should go. I'm sorry."

Before she could move, Bill clutched her forearm
again, hard. "Look at me," he said. When she did, he
continued, "I'll go back to that fucking house with you if
that's what you need for closure. Get one last look at it,
walk through it, whatever you need to do. And then you
need to move on. I'll even take you for a beer after our
little memory lane tour, how does that sound?"

Sifting through her chaotic thoughts, Julie nodded.
"Yeah, okay."

Truth was she didn't know what she'd expected.
She'd simply made the decision, jumped into her car and
drove. It sounded like as much of a solution as anything
else.

She would face her demons, and she would find
closure.

Yeah. Right.

As they pulled up in Bill's Chevy, Julie's eyes flicked
instantly to that damned front window. And, like the eye
of some malicious specter, the hole in its center stared
back.

The expanse of snow-coated field behind the manor
looked mockingly pastoral. The only sound was wind.

"Jesus Christ, Bill," Julie said. "We repaired that window decades ago. *Decades* ago."

Bill, too tall for his own good, tilted his head down and squinted to get a better look. An expression of boyish fear crossed his face, open mouth and glistening wide eyes, but he quickly gathered himself and shrugged. "Some nasty vandal, probably. I'll have to get it fixed again, file a police report. Because, shit, I don't have enough on my plate already."

He eased the truck into the driveway and parked. As soon as he unbuckled his seatbelt, he pulled his smokes out of his jacket pocket, knocked one out and sparked up.

Still unable to turn away from the hole in the window, Julie extended her hand and said, "Can I bum one?"

Bill fixed her with a look of disbelief. "You don't smoke."

"I know," Julie said, still holding out her hand.

Bill shook his head, bemused, and passed her a cigarette. Hand trembling, she stuck it between her lips.

"Inhale," he said as he extended his lighter.

She did, then coughed violently.

Bill grunted a laugh, cracked open his door and stepped onto the driveway. Chilly winter wind flooded the truck cabin. Julie followed him out, pulling again on her smoke. She coughed less this time, relishing the tingly rush in her head.

Bill offered her a shaky smile. "Want to finish that before we head inside?"

Julie cast her eyes toward the house, a foreboding and lightless outline etched against the night sky, and she shook her head. She took one more drag, her deepest, and tossed the remainder into the snow. "No," she said. "I just want to get this over with. Whatever's in there, I want it to know I'm onto it. It's high time it moves on to someone else."

Bill smiled around the smoldering cigarette balanced between his teeth. "Mind if I finish?"

Julie shook her head no. She jammed her hands into her pockets and took a step closer to the manor, all darkly staring windows and closed doors. Her breath fogged the night air as she replied, "Go ahead." She crunched up the driveway, drawing nearer to the entrance.

From behind, she heard Bill mutter, "fuck it," followed by the sound of his boots clopping snow as he jogged to meet her.

They made their way to the front steps, walking in tandem, and before either of them could say a hesitant word or pose a question (*Why are we doing this? What are we going to solve?*), Julie's hand was on the doorknob.

"Might need a key to get in, sis," Bill said. His face swooped in beside her, wafting tobacco scents. He nudged her aside, stuck his key in the lock and pushed the door open. The foyer looked vast and black.

Julie filled her lungs with breath, offered herself a mental *You can do this*, and stepped inside. Her boots echoed on the hardwood, filling the vast space with sound, stirring memories. Bill closed the door with a resounding thud, and everything was silent.

"Right," Julie said. Her eyes followed the staircase upward, into the deeper blackness. "What now?" She turned to face her brother, whose face was frozen in a grim smile. She put her hands on her hips and leaned in toward him. "Bill? What do we do now?"

Bill's smile didn't waver. "We say hi to whatever's been fucking with you, and we tell it to take a hike. That sounds about right, doesn't it?"

Julie flicked her eyes across her brother's expression, becoming suddenly conscious of her own heartbeat, a blunt force rhythm that seemed to resonate in her throat and reverberate all the way up to her ears.

"Why are you smiling?" she blurted.

Without answering, Bill strode toward the staircase. His movement was stilted, erratic, his stiff arms swinging at his sides like he was performing some mockery of a military march. "Follow me," he called.

Julie could no longer deny the menacing vibration she remembered all too well from childhood, rearing its head in the space between her consciousness and unconsciousness. It was the familiar sense that signaled the arrival of an imposter.

She ignored her brother and rushed down the small hallway toward the unlit and empty bathroom. Her face was reflected in the mirror above the sink, big eyes glowing fear even in the murk.

"No, this is wrong," she said, stopping mid-stride. She wheeled back around and ran for the front door.

She gripped the doorknob, but it wouldn't turn. Then it fully descended: the presence of a thing that imitated domestic familiarity, the palpable knowledge that some force was in the room with her, some awful gaze leering from a nonexistent face. Her heartbeat was becoming assaultive, nearly deafening, an echoey and brutal sound that filled her skull.

"No," she said. "No."

A grating, crunching noise carried from upstairs, like something heavy dragging over broken glass.

"Bill?" she called, uselessly, feeling idiotic and small. She backed away from the sealed door and ran for the stairs, making her way toward the sound. She called her brother's name again, taking the steps two at a time, doing her best to suppress her terror and failing in the profoundest way.

Whoever or whatever she was calling, it was not Bill, just as surely as whoever or whatever had brought her here was not her brother. The thing had become stronger than she'd ever imagined. Maybe it had wormed its way into her consciousness, willing this insane trip into being. And she'd been stupid enough to fall for it.

She arrived at the loft, where she'd once stood as a child and beheld a rock surrounded by a spray of window-shards, and her fear tore its way through her abdomen and exploded from her mouth. It was a desperate scream, devoid of reason and control, splitting through her false veneer of strength.

A giant pink and yellow-blotted finger was wriggling through the hole in the window, pushing through the jagged remnants of glass and dripping huge globules of blood on the wood. It twitched and forced its way toward her, its monolithic fingernail swimming into her vision like a monster's eye.

Julie fell onto her ass, sending a shockwave of pain up her spine.

The giant finger writhed in front of her like something sentient, its flesh still ripping along the broken glass. The nicotine stains gathered around its knuckle looked like gargantuan blots of yellow paint.

After an interminable stretch of grinding and squelchy effort, it retracted, dragging blood and slivers, then disappeared into the night.

Julie sat, trying to will her pulse back to a sane pace, her breath catching at the base of her throat. An awful stillness descended. Shaking, she propped herself back up and stepped toward the red-stained window.

What faced her was not the night sky, but a too familiar vista of off-green paint catching lamplight. It was broken by a blotch of stark black and white—the massive angle of a woman's elbow. There was no mistaking the rare Patti Smith poster that had caught stupid Todd's gaze last night, the cover of *Radio Ethiopia* blown up to the size of an IMAX screen.

Off to the side, a wall of plaid heaved with giant breath. It was Bill's shirt. But the thing living inside that mountain of fabric was not her brother. The plaid-clad body dissolved, turning a grotesque gray before fading into soft pink. Once reformed, the body moved again. The new, immense abdomen glided by the window, displaying stretch marks and a mole that Julie recognized with instant and unthinkable dread. It was her own bare stomach, upsized to mammoth proportions. Giant Julie was crossing Julie's bedroom, seemingly indifferent to the built-to-scale miniature house on her desktop.

And Julie, mouth agape and body trembling, was trapped inside Mini McDonagh Manor. She wanted so badly to scream, but something was pressing hard against her mouth, trapping the noise inside. The thing was back, and it was making no more pretensions.

"You're home again," it said, the words filtered through some off-tone aberration that sounded like her own voice garbled by Bill's.

And then it pulled Julie back, away from the sights that had paralyzed her with fear. Soon everything was dark, and she thought, *Help me, Mommy*.

Mom was nowhere to be found, but her father's voice spoke up from the shadows. "Julie," he said. "We've got an awful lot to discuss. Let's go down to the cellar."

Quickly, Something Familiar

... Chris Patrick Carolan

Taber. Yorkton. East Bumblefuck. The name of the town didn't matter, they all had the same bar. Dark caves of cinderblock or red brick, wooden tables yellowed by the nicotine of cigarettes smoked long ago, sticky floors, and the heady potpourri of stale sweat and staler beer. The only way to tell the difference from week to week was whether the neon sign on the wall was flogging Budweiser or Heineken. The same Saturday-night assortment of Chads and Kyles rolled in from the fields or the rigs or whatever source of income happened to be nearest to town. Fueled by cheap happy-hour beers and lonely weeks away, flush with cash, they infiltrated the dance floor, doing their best to pick up the townie girls with names like Jenna, Brenna, and the occasional McKenna. They all danced the same dance.

Amanda Kaine's bass guitar hung low at her hip. The footlights lining the front of the tiny stage were perfectly angled to blind her if she wasn't careful. She kept her head low and dragged a series of sludgy A and E notes out of the bass. The Low-Key Lowlifes were halfway into a Smashing Pumpkins song.

"Who wants honey?" Wesley whined into the mic. "As long as there's some money." His Billy Corgan impression was far from perfect, but the Chads and Jennas on the dance floor didn't care. The music on stage was necessary but secondary to the mating ritual. Cover songs were the order of the evening, and the covers had better be songs they knew and wanted to hear. If they weren't, beer bottles would fly. Even "Cherub Rock" was pushing it.

"Tell me all of your secrets. Cannot help but believe this is true…"

A figure at the far end of the bar caught Amanda's eye.

"Let me out," Wesley sang.

He was tall and lean and bathed in the Heineken sign's light, and his gaunt face took on a ghastly greenish hue like the yolk of an overboiled egg.

"Let me out…"

The dark suit the stranger wore looked like something out of the 1800s, a stark contrast from the Fox Racing and "Keep Calm and Chive On" T-shirts that were the uniform of the Chads.

"Let me out!"

He struck Amanda as a man out of place, out of time.

The song came to its frenetic, feedback-fuzzed end.

"Okay, we're going to get Mandy Kaine up here for this next one," Wesley said, gesturing to Amanda to take the microphone. "Be nice to her, okay?"

Mandy Kaine. Her high school nickname would've been a great stage name if she had been part of the '70s punk scene or a '90s riot grrrl band. She had played up the nickname as a teenager, too, wearing red-striped clothes and dabbing peppermint essential oil on her neck and wrists instead of perfume. But that had been a decade ago, now. She stepped up to the mic, adjusted the stand. Wesley was a good six inches taller than she was and never remembered it when he stepped aside. She had long since stopped rolling her eyes or sighing about it.

It was the kind of gig where the audience tolerated one original song after every four or five familiar covers. Of all the songs Amanda had written, "If These Walls Could Talk" was one of her favorites, an upbeat song with sad lyrics about youthful discovery and a very real heartbreak, now also more than ten years in the past. The girl in the song was long gone, but Amanda still felt a pang every time she sang the words. Not that anyone here was paying any attention to the lyrics.

No, that wasn't quite true, she realized as she came to the end of the first verse. In that keen way one knows when they're being watched, Amanda felt eyes on her through the length of the song. It wasn't just the audience. Without looking to the far end of the bar, she knew the gaze belonged to the skinny guy under the green light. Instead of making her nervous, though, his intense scrutiny emboldened her. She reached deep as though tapping into a well she hadn't known existed, pouring more of herself into the song than she had ever done before. The rest of the Low-Key Lowlifes, in response, played with a grace and skill well beyond their usual measure.

The final notes drew a smattering of applause, even as the band looked to each other with eyes wide, aware that the performance had been transcendent. Amanda looked up, searched the room for the skinny guy in the suit, but he was nowhere to be seen. Wesley tapped her on the shoulder, and she returned to her place on his right.

Quickly, a wise man had once said, *follow the unknown with something more familiar*. On the drums, Aaron tapped out a measured beat, launching the Low-Key Lowlifes into AC/DC's "Back in Black." The dance floor swelled. A one-man mosh pit swirled about, windmilling his arm like Pete Townshend with a case of the staggers.

Amanda sighed inwardly and plucked the bass strings.

It was that kind of show.

Waxy yellow light cast by aging phosphorus bulbs filled the parking lot, drawing moths and other insects in the calm summer night. The moths and lights buzzed together. A warm breeze carried the sharp scent of a feedlot from somewhere nearby. Wherever it was, it was too far to hear the cattle lowing. Amanda didn't remember passing a feedlot on the way into town. Maybe the parking lot behind the bar just smelled like piss. It wouldn't be the first time.

The street beyond had that stillness one only finds in small towns at midnight, when the shops have all been closed for hours and most of the townies are at home in their beds. It would soon be broken when the bartenders sounded last call, then corralled the unruly mob out into the night. The fights would start when a particular segment of the male population found themselves on the sidewalk, companionless at closing time.

Amanda and the Low-Key Lowlifes planned to have the van packed and be on their way before it got to that hour. Wesley and Aaron were carting the amplifiers and drum kit out in pieces, making trips back and forth from the van. Colby, the Lowlifes' second guitarist, had wandered off somewhere for a smoke, as he usually did when there was lifting to be done.

The plaintive keening of a lone coyote broke the quiet, a long howl followed by a series of quick yips. Amanda's father had called them "singing dogs" when she was little, and she always smiled at the memory when she heard their song in the night. To her, the coyote's call was a wistful invitation to meet and run together in the moonlight.

For now, she waited with the van, alone, keeping watch over the band's equipment. *Not that I could do much about it if anyone actually wanted to steal our gear*, she thought.

She heard the whistling before she saw the figure, recognized her own song in the notes. Just as keenly, she was aware the sounds of the night–coyote, buzzing insects and parking lot lights–had ceased. The skinny man in the dark suit appeared as if out of nowhere, the bassline of "If These Walls Could Talk" heralding his arrival.

"I wonder if I might have a word, Miss Kaine?"

Up close his face was all angles and shadow and, even now, away from the Heineken sign, his skin somehow held that greenish tinge. That aside, Amanda decided he was not altogether unhandsome.

"Who are you?"

"Call me Mister Skin," the stranger hissed.

"Mister Skin?" She fought back a chuckle. "Did you make that up yourself?"

He ignored the jab. "Why do you hide in the background of your band, Miss Kaine?"

"What do you mean?"

"Every original song," he said, "you're the one singing."

"Well, you're not wrong." Amanda shrugged and made a vague gesture toward the bar full of Chads and Jennas. "But my songs aren't what *they're* here for. This isn't that kind of show."

"More's the pity," Mister Skin said. "Do not give what is holy to dogs, nor cast your pearls before swine."

"Something like that, yeah."

He smiled, the corners of his mouth pulling back to a point that would've made Conrad Veidt envious. "I have a message from your sister," he said.

"I don't have a sister."

"Your Otherself, then, if you prefer the term."

"I have no idea what you're talking about."

Mister Skin sighed. "You people never do."

Amanda sniffed. "What's that supposed to mean?"

"I've travelled an impossible distance to speak with you, Miss Kaine, and yet I've scarcely gone anywhere at all, if you take my meaning." He paused and studied her face. "No, I suppose you don't, at that, but I'll try to explain. My time here grows short. You see, I am but an Envoy, one who walks between worlds, going anywhere and anywhen my services are required."

"Between worlds?"

"Different threads of existence, realities unspooling parallel to but distinct from this one." He paused for a moment, a contemplative look on his face. "How much do you know about quantum theory?"

"Nothing at all."

"Have you ever seen Star Trek?"

"Of course."

"Well, then, think of it as one of those episodes where Spock is evil and has a beard."

"So, like a parallel universe," she said, arching an eyebrow, "and you have Star Trek there?"

"Some things are transuniversal," Mister Skin explained. "Not every universe had a Gene Roddenberry, but most that did had a Star Trek as well. In half of those threads, though, Jeffrey Hunter played Captain Pike for five seasons."

"Okay," Amanda said. "I can go along with that."

He blinked. "You believe me?"

"Sure," Amanda shrugged. "I've seen some weird shit driving back and forth across the prairies. But what's this about an Otherself?"

"Finally, we come to the core of the matter! Your Otherself is the version of you from another thread,"

Mister Skin said. "In this case, one specific thread with one specific Otherself. Her world is dying, as worlds tend to do. Worlds end all the time, you know, but you people are only ever aware of it when it's the one you're living in. At any rate, of the countless Amanda Kaines in existence, you're the only one who can help her."

"Why me?" Her eyes narrowed as she scanned his face, seeking any hint of some other, unspoken motive. It wouldn't be the first time some random at a bar had spun her a crazy story, though this was crazier than most. "I'm no one special."

"Threads of reality are split off from each other by certain events or decisions. There's a notion in quantum theory that every choice creates separate threads, but for trifling things the splits tend to repair themselves without any intervention." He held up his hand and spread his fingers wide. "Say you're choosing your lunch from five meals on a menu, there's potential to create five different threads based on your choice. But it doesn't really matter to the universe if you choose chicken fingers or a tuna sandwich, or if you get up and go to a different restaurant altogether. Those tiny schisms re-twine themselves without notice and the thread continues to unspool." He closed his hand into a fist. "Bigger decisions make bigger changes. If someone decided to become a nurse or a social worker instead of, say, and actuary, that creates a very different thread. One where a lot more people have been helped than would've been otherwise. Several different lives."

"Sort of like It's a Wonderful Life."

"I don't know what that means," Mister Skin said.

"Okay, well, that still doesn't explain what any of this has to do with me."

"The Amanda Kaine I'm talking about comes from a thread created by something that happened in your past, but not hers. The thread she follows was split off from your own, and took her down a different path in life. You're the only one who's..." he paused, searching for the right word. "Compatible." Sweat beaded on his brow, his skin taking on a dull, grayish pallor.

"Why doesn't she just come to this world, like you did?"

"She's unable to cross the threshold. I'm rather, ah... *unique* in my ability to do so. An accident of my birth that set me on a thread of my own, separate from all others." A pensive look crossed his face and he held up his hands, which trembled. "A blessing and a curse, really. And even I can't maintain my form here for more than a few hours."

Amanda looked around, suddenly keenly aware of the absence of her bandmates. "Where are the guys? They should've been back out here by now."

"Another one of my talents, Miss Kaine." Mister Skin spread his hands wide. "I've sort of paused things while we spoke, to ensure we were not interrupted." His face twisted into a pained grimace. "As I said before, though, my time here grows short. Look to meet your Otherself on the night of the solstice." He staggered, threw one hand against the side of the van to steady himself. "The threshold will be narrowest then." He seemed to go fuzzy around the edges, like someone in an old instant photograph.

The coyote's call pierced the silence, but it was a rough, staccato sort of sound. "You still haven't told me why you care," Amanda said. Her stomach twitched and gurgled as she realized whatever it was that Mister Skin was using to pause time was slipping. "What's in it for you?"

"I'm an Envoy, as I said," Mister Skin said. "My own thread is shapeless, without substance, but I can cross into the physical plane when needed. My task is to re-entwine threads that never should have split apart in the first place. There's always an instability in both threads when that happens, you see, but sometimes we can help with that. I can't change the past–no one can–but I can help restore certain things torn asunder." He gasped, looking as though he was about to vomit, but continued. "Know this, Miss Kaine... a part of you was lost when the threads were split, and the instability that's tearing that thread apart is here as well. I can feel it in the air. Your Otherself can help make it right," his features grew more indistinct, "if you let her. As for what's in it for me," he added, smiling, "I got to hear music tonight. That's payment enough."

The coyote howled a long and unbroken song. The lights above flickered and buzzed along with the swarming insects, and Amanda turned her head toward the sudden return of sound.

When she turned back, Mister Skin was gone.

Long roads stretched between drive-by towns, high beams lighting the way home in the pre-dawn dark. Amanda drove while Wesley dozed in the passenger seat. Aaron was stretched out on the bench seat behind, with Colby wrapped up in a sleeping bag on the floor in the back beside the amplifiers. The worst spot in the van was his penance for disappearing during loading, but he never complained about it.

The quiet gave Amanda time to think.

The summer solstice was six days away. Another Saturday, playing another gig in another small town.

Mister Skin. The things he had been saying made little sense to her, had seemed impossible, but the things he had done had seemed so real. Pausing time, vanishing before her eyes, somehow making her and the band play better than they ever had before. If he could do those things... maybe there was some truth to his claims?

The week dragged by in a blur. Office cubicle greys gave way to lunch-hour food court trays, which gave way to the small condo on the fourteenth floor. She had furnished the unit in faux mid-century modern, her books on white shelves arranged by the color of their spines rather than filing them alphabetically or by subject.

This week, it felt like someone else's home.

Nothing had changed. Every piece of furniture, every book or record or scrap of clothing was exactly as she had left it, exactly as it had been when she had left for the small town where she had met Mister Skin. Yet the uncanny feeling of being somehow in the wrong place persisted. She slept fitfully; thought she saw things out of the corner of her eye. Even the water out of the tap tasted ever so slightly off.

I'm just tired, she thought. Working too much, maybe.

Only singing and playing the bass felt right, whether during rehearsal with the Low-Key Lowlifes or on her own at home. The music, the lyrics… that was home.

Saturday, we're on the road again, she thought as she strummed alone in her room. Long roads drawing straight lines between patchwork fields, pastures, and fields dotted with pumpjacks turning in their ceaseless rhythm lay before her and whatever encounter Mister Skin had foretold. *Where is it this week? Lethbridge? Wayne? Saskatoon?*

Does it matter?

The mirror in a truck stop washroom halfway between Red Deer and Saskatoon would've been the last place Amanda might have expected to meet her Otherself, had she thought to expect it there at all. Yet there the other Amanda stood, looking every inch a rock star. It wasn't simply her clothes, hair, and makeup, though those were all fantastic. No, the other Amanda armed herself with a will and determination Amanda thought might be buried deep somewhere inside herself, if she could only find the key to unlock the door.

"Really?" Amanda asked once she had overcome the surprise. "The bathroom?"

"This is where the threshold is thinnest right now," the other Amanda explained.

"This is insane," Amanda said. "What do I even call you?"

"I've always preferred Mandy."

Of course.

"So, how does this work?"

"I can't cross the threshold into your world," Mandy said, "at least, not the way Mister Skin did. That's why I need you."

Something in the way Mandy said that sounded sinister, but Amanda found herself unable to step back from the mirror. The mirror glass seemed to melt away, and the room felt as though the air was being slowly sucked out through the frame into whatever gulf existed between the worlds. Amanda held her breath.

Somehow weightless and insubstantial, Mandy drifted through the mirror frame.

"My body can't cross the divide," she said, her voice now sounding very far away. "I need you to breathe me in."

Breathe her in? Amanda thought. This wasn't part of the deal.

"Please, Amanda," Mandy pleaded. "I won't survive long on this side if you don't take me in."

Mandy touched a ghostly finger to Amanda's lips. She tasted like peppermint.

Memories cascaded over Amanda like a river, taking her back. To the girl who first called her Mandy Kaine,

who had first told her she had a nice voice. The silly
songs they had written together and laughed about. The
hockey boys who threw full cans of Coke from their cars
while shouting "*dyke bitches!*" and how they had run
home and cried. The small town they had both left
behind, and the happy year and a half together in
Vancouver before it had all fallen apart.

Laurel. Beautiful Laurel, with her black hair and
always-drowsy brown eyes. So much of Amanda had
been closed off when she had left.

"I know. I knew her, too," Mandy said. "It was
different for us, though. We had a lot more time
together, after the bad stretch in Vancouver. We made it
through, though, and she built me up every day. She was
my rock." Sadness showed on her face for just a
moment, then was replaced once more by confident,
steely resolve. "My Laurel is gone now, too, but I can
help with what's missing."

Tears standing in her eyes, Amanda opened her
mouth and breathed deeply.

Amanda walked out of the washroom and headed to the
corner booth where Wesley, Aaron, and Colby sat with
sandwiches and coffee. Eyes lingered on her as she
walked across the restaurant; truckers and farmers,
families, the busboy, and waitress. She held the room. It
didn't feel weird. It was weird, how weird it didn't feel.

She settled in, looking past her plate, past the guys.
The window looked out over the parking lot, a sizable

gray gravel field with pickup trucks and eighteen-wheelers and camper vans and RVs lined up in orderly fashion, as though laid out by some fastidious, enormous toddler. Past the trucks, a view of the highway beyond, ripening wheat swaying like the waves of some golden ocean. A murder of crows rose up from the field in a flurry of wings, squawking at some calamity Amanda hadn't seen.

Tonight's show was just a little up the road, in another nameless bar in another nameless town. But tomorrow, and next week?

She sipped her coffee. That highway was a long road.

"Let's give the Chads something different tonight, okay?" she said. "All originals. I promise, they'll love it." The guys looked at her in mild surprise, shrugged as one, and went back to eating.

She smiled, feeling a confidence she hadn't felt in years. It was true. Something had been given back to her.

"And call me Mandy."

The Frostlings
… Chris Marrs

I contemplated the cabin before me. Fluffy flakes of snow–dry compared to the sloppy wet West Coast flakes I was used to–fell all around. They stuck to my hair and eyelashes. Their blanket muffled sound. In the quiet, I felt like the only person left in a silent, white world. We'd only ever come here in the summer. Now it had its first winter visitor.

"Come look, Mommy, I made a snow angel," Maya said, glee in her voice.

"You're not here," I whispered as my womb cramped, a phantom spasm. "You're still in Vancouver with your father."

For a moment my daughter in the pink snowsuit stood waving at me to come see; in the next the snow swirled her away. Trembling, whether from cold, exhaustion, or sorrow, I didn't know, I gathered the grocery bag of meagre supplies I'd picked up on my way through Stettler and my suitcase.

The front door opened into a small kitchen. A counter in front of me, a stove and fridge huddled together on the left. Beside the door and under the window dressed in faded curtains crouched a wood table with three mismatched chairs. A cribbage board and a deck of cards lay on the window sill. Cozy. My Aunt Hazel and Uncle Peter used to sit here drinking beer and playing crib while the summer sunshine filled the room. Now frost limned the glass and a chill hung in the air.

In keeping with our agreement to keep contact to a minimum, I flashed off a text to Greg to let him and Maya know I arrived safe. It wasn't that he didn't want to talk to me. I was here to recuperate, and my counsellor thought bare minimum contact while I did so would be beneficial in the long run. I grudgingly went along with her.

I banged the snow off my boots, removed them, then hung my coat on the hook behind the door. Picking up my suitcase to avoid tracking in the snow clinging to the wheels, I went through the archway into the living room. Unadorned wood panel walls darkened the room. Even the light coming from the picture window refused to brighten it. A fireplace sat along the far wall. I'd been warned it was the main source of heat but that I would find a space heater in the cellar. Without my jacket, the cold nipped at me for attention. My immediate plan became to unpack a sweater and get some heat going.

Outside, the wind kicked up. It moaned through the eaves and threw snow onto the windowpane. The clothing I brought filled three of the five dresser drawers and four closet hangers. I set my toiletries on top of the dresser and shoved the suitcase under the double bed. Hiking up the sleeves of my fuzzy hoodie, I went back to the living room to tackle the heat situation. One smoke-filled room later, I discovered how to work the flue, and, voilà, a small, crackling fire chewed at the logs. I tossed in a few crumpled balls of old newspaper in hopes of bringing it to a roar, then closed the metal curtain.

Night had fallen during my tussle with the fire and along with it came a growling stomach. I put away the groceries–enough for two days–and set about making tomato soup and grilled cheese. While the soup warmed and the sandwich fried, I checked my phone for a message from Greg. I didn't expect a reply. My heart leapt when I spotted his name among the social media notifications then sank when I read it.

Thanks for letting me know. We miss you already. I saw Kevin yesterday.

My breath caught and my heart stuttered. I powered down the cell instead of scrolling through notifications to find the rest of his message. The anxiety always waiting to pounce threatened to tighten my chest when I thought of reading what he had to say about my brother. The first bubbles roiling at the surface of the soup became a welcome distraction.

Once the soup was boiling, I poured it into a bowl, added pepper and butter, put the grilled cheese on a napkin, and brought the meal into the living room. Sitting at the little kitchen table without my brother, aunt and uncle felt too lonely.

During the summers we spent here, every meal–except for the rare picnic or trip into Stettler for dinner–happened at the table. Uncle Peter would regale us with tales of his youth while Aunt Hazel pretended to be scandalized. However, when his tale ended, she always followed up with a tale more scandalous than his. Kevin

and I laughed at her stories until we clutched our bellies
and fought not to fall from our chairs. Now, Uncle Peter
resided in an urn, which in turn sat on the dresser in
Aunt Hazel's assisted living home.

The paltry fire had grown while I made dinner and
now tossed enough heat to warm the room. A wing-back
chair with a footstool before it invited me to sit. I popped
up my slipper-clad feet and placed my sandwich on the
little table beside the chair. While I dipped one sandwich
half into soup, the fire roasted the soles of my slippers.
The toasted cheese and soup tasted like childhood.
Outside the wind shrieked by the window and howled
around the corners.

Cold winter sunlight streamed through the seam of the
drapes when I awoke the next morning. A giggle faded
into the distance and took the sliver of a nightmare with
it, a reoccurring nightmare I'd hoped I left behind in
Vancouver. I'd come here to heal from something that
felt so real but wasn't, not to drag it here with me.
Thinking of the nightmare reminded me of the text from
my husband the night before.

I picked up the phone from the nightstand, then set it
back down. It'd keep until after coffee. I tossed off the
covers and instantly regretted it. Cold air rushed in and
puckered my skin into goosebumps. Teeth threatening to
chatter, I added a sweater over my pajamas and an extra
pair of socks under the slippers. I made a mental note to

find the space heater, if only to keep the bedroom warm at night.

Once I lit the fire–first attempt, yay me–I opened the drapes and squinted from the glare of sunshine hitting brilliant white snow. Last night's storm left a fresh blanket of the stuff. About a foot judging by the pile on the roof of my car. The road remained invisible, and I wondered if it'd be plowed today or if I'd have to wait until tomorrow to head into Stettler. Freezing air wafted from the window. Along its edges frost feathers curled and twisted into random patterns. I reclosed the drapes to keep the heat from escaping.

I got the coffee going and its warm scent filled the kitchen. Before the brew completed, I poured a mug and brought it to the wingback chair. I savoured the first sip of heaven and cognisance. It provided the chemically induced jolt I needed. I powered my cell back up to a chorus of pings and dings of incoming texts and social media notifications. I ignored them all and focused on finding Greg's.

...He said he hopes you find the peace you are looking for and to remember it's not your fault. Maya and I agree. Love u

I swear if I hear my family–especially my brother–say I'm not to blame one more time, I'll scream. Okay, I won't but, if not for Maya, I might seriously consider not returning to Vancouver. Pushing the family drama and incident out of my mind, I sent off: *Tell him will do, for you all. <3.* I disregarded the other messages and notifications and powered the cell down again. On the drive through the mountains, I'd decided to take a break from social media, and, well, everything. Too many *you're in our thoughts; sending prayers; hugs to you in this difficult time; let me know if you need anything* texts and comments. At first, I *liked* and *loved* every response. Now they felt like a chore, an emotionally fatiguing draining chore. At some point, the comments and texted started to sound false, more like platitudes than meaningful well wishes. I stoked the fire and went to refill my coffee and start my breakfast.

A late start for me. By now I'd have put in an hour at my desk. The normal scramble of getting Maya ready for kindergarten, a Pilates class, and the drive during rush hour would be behind me. The city traffic would have driven me bonkers. Cyclists zooming around not paying attention to the road rules, making me curse them. The drive home at night–late, always late, always another project to complete or start before leaving–a reprieve from the crazy-making morning. Coming home to Greg nagging about how my boss took advantage of me and it was cutting into our family life.

By the time I was caffeinated, fed, and showered, the snowplow still hadn't made an appearance, so Stettler wasn't an option. Not for this West Coast chicken anyway. I could handle an inch of snow but not a foot. Figuring now was as good a time as any to search for the space heater, I opened the door to the cellar. Frigid air greeted me. I closed the door.

I put on my coat and gloves and tried again. The wooden steps creaked under my weight. At the small landing before the steps switchbacked, I paused. The dark crept up like tendrils. Icy tendrils. I turned around and went back up. Cellar 2, me 0. I went to get my cell.

I turned on the cell–more notifications and texts to be dismissed pinged–and hit the flashlight icon. Once more down the steps. The light banished the dark enough for me to continue. A foot from the bottom of the steps dangled a pull chain. My slippers gritted on the dirt floor but I wasn't going back up a third time for my boots. I pulled the chain. Weak yellow light spread across the room.

The cellar sprawled the length and width of the cabin. Random roots–layered with cobwebs–broke through the stone walls here and there. I squirmed at the webbing but they appeared old and, hopefully, absent of spiders. A dented yet rust-free washer and drier lurked in a corner. An apartment-sized freezer sat beside them and a stack of fresh firewood beside the freezer. I must remember to thank cousin Seth for it later, as I'm positive that was his doing. If I remembered correctly, Uncle Peter's workbench was near the back. I went deeper into the cellar, keeping the cell flashlight on to supplement the dim lighting.

Dust covered a vise attached to the otherwise empty workspace. The shelves held the various bric-a-brac common to a summer cabin. Gardening tools–a trowel, hand rake, and pruning shears–mason jars of nuts, bolts, and nails, and the hammer, screwdriver, and wrench of the minimalist do-it-yourselfer. And, voilà, a small space heater. I pulled the dusty thing from the shelf. There was a loud *thwock* and I jumped.

A children's storybook had landed on the workbench. The space heater had been sitting on top of it and when I pulled it down the book came too. I brushed the light layer of grime off to read the title: *The Frostlings*.

Summer nights filled my memory: Kevin and me lying on sleeping bags in the tent, front flap open to watch the fireflies dance above the grass, waiting for Aunt Hazel to come read our bedtime story. We requested *The Frostlings* so many times I'm sure Aunt Hazel had it memorized. And now here it was, a reminder of the carefree summer days of childhood. It felt wrong to abandon the book to the cellar. I brought it upstairs with me and the heater.

Carefully I wiped down the space heater with a rag I found under the kitchen sink. Dust flew. I sneezed. Satisfied I'd done all I could, I plugged it in. It whirred away to warm the bedroom with scorched-dust-scented heat while I sat propped in bed to keep an eye on it until the dust burned off the filaments. I wiped down *The Frostlings* with the same rag. Its pages were a little swollen, as if it'd gotten wet at some point. The illustrations, however, stood out crisp and clear like the book was new. I turned to the first page.

Out of the woods, through the fields, and down the lane the frostlings come to tap-tap-tap on your window pane.

After this first page Aunt Hazel would tap-tap our noses.

Frosty loops of feathers, swirls of wings, twists of leaves grow beneath their fingers as they giggle into their sleeves.

Of course, we'd giggle into our sleeves as she turned the page.

If you shall wake while they are drawing do not let them see you or something from you they will take.

A baby doll, a ball, or your big fluffy cat. Oh no, you wouldn't like that!

By the end of the story—when the frostlings had taken away all the toys and the children went off in search of them—Kevin and I would be clutching each other's hands. When she was finished, Aunt Hazel always snapped the book shut. We would jump, then laugh like loons and demand she read it again. Looking back, the rise of fear and tension followed by the sudden release was what drove us to ask for it every night.

Out of the dark recesses of my brain an untrustworthy voice rose: *They ended up taking more than toys. You shouldn't have peeked.* I shuddered and told myself no one had taken Maya and Greg away. They were safe in Vancouver while I came here—ran away—to find the me I recently lost.

The thunderous scraping of the snowplow pulled me from my dark thoughts. I closed the book and set it on the nightstand. Outside, the snow crested and broke like a wave as the plow cleared the way. An escape.

My little SUV slipped a smidge on the scrim of snow covering the road as I turned into the driveway. On the drive back from Stettler the flatness of the prairies struck me as it never had as a child. The land sprawled until it met the horizon. The expanse of dirt coupled with the huge sky above–laden with grey snow clouds–felt claustrophobic in a way the mountains and ocean never had.

I dropped the grocery bags on the kitchen table. Shaking the snow from my hair, I unzipped my coat. Chilly air rushed in. I shivered. I'd let the fire burn down before heading out but kept the space heater on until it was time to go. It shouldn't be this cold in here already– I'd only been gone an hour. Instead of removing my jacket or putting the groceries away, I moved toward the living room intending to turn on the space heater. I froze in the entrance.

The living room sparkled with a coating of frost, from thin icy leaves blooming across the panel walls to the sugar dust on the wingback chair. Wing shapes and flowers swooped over the open window. A smattering of little icy footprints trailed from the window to the bedroom and back out again. My heart shuddered and pounded and my breath sat at the edge of a scream as I stepped into the room to look closer.

As soon as I crossed the threshold, the living room reverted to its natural frost-free state. The open window was now closed. Only the frosty decorations patterning the single-paned glass remained. Fear made me giggle until I sank onto the floor and cried. Big, ugly sobs wracked my frame, and at the same time I felt lighter. Time passed, but how much, I didn't know. My cold numb bum brought me back as my sobs turned to hiccups, then to quiet sniffles. Without questioning the reason behind my breakdown, I rose on autopilot to put away the groceries.

I focused entirely on dealing with the groceries, then I hopped into the shower to dispel the deep chill in my bones from sitting on the floor. Under the hot spray, I allowed the earlier weirdness space in my head. Tired, repressed stress, too far from home, and missing Maya and Greg: they all contributed to the hallucination. The footprints and frost I explained away by my recent trip into nostalgia with *The Frostlings*. *But the footprints in frost. So tiny. So like a little girl's.* I harrumphed, then told the empty bathroom of course the prints were little; the frostlings were small creatures. The voice didn't reply. Shutting up the voice–another win for me–I relaxed and luxuriated under the hot spray until my skin pruned and the water turned cold.

Back in my pajamas and slippers, hair wrapped in a towel, I popped a pizza in the oven. For the first time in a long time I felt content. I believed things were smoothing out, that the cathartic ugly cry opened the door to healing. Sure, it took a vivid hallucination to take me there, but I was confident it was exactly what I needed, why I came here. By the time I returned to Vancouver, I'd be back to my old self.

Nightfall brought another blizzard with it. I returned to my spot–I thought of the wing-backed chair as my spot now, owning it–with a plate of pizza and glass of pop. Wind whistled down the chimney to twist the fire into a tornado of sparks. A crack echoed through the living room like a gunshot. I jumped. Another crack, then the logs shifted and settled.

The sense of loneliness permeated the atmosphere: my loneliness, the cabin's, both perhaps. I glanced at the darkened cell on the little table, a napkin half covering its face. Not too late to call. Maya didn't go to bed for another hour. I missed her voice. And it wouldn't be like I was really ignoring our agreement; it had been a day since my last message. Steeling against the barrage of notifications, I turned it on and called home.

After five empty rings the voicemail clicked on. Greg's voice filled the space followed by mine, then Maya's and back to Greg: *Hi you've reached Greg, Cass, and Maya* (her giggles floated out like bubbles). *You know what to do.* I smiled at the silly family greeting while I disconnected the call. No matter how many times Greg and I recorded the message we weren't able to get Maya to stop giggling. I fired off a text. *Tried calling but guess you two rascals are out. Love you both to pieces.* Then promptly turned the phone off.

Frozen lips pressed against my cheek.

My eyes shot open. Little feet pitter-pattered out of the room in time to the *whomp-thump* of my heart. On the nightstand, my cell buzzed and buzzed. In the distance, a siren wailed. Breath coming in ragged chunks, I scrabbled for the phone. My fingertips brushed it, sending it skittering onto the floor. Giggles came from the kitchen. I leaned out of bed and ran a hand back and forth along the floor until I touched the cool plastic of the phone case. I picked it up. The buzzing stopped. I hit the home button hoping to see a missed call from Greg. Nothing. The front door clicked closed.

I sat up. A scream in my throat and pulse thundering in my ears. Grey light bathed the bedroom. The greasy fear-sweat coating my face rapidly cooled in the chilly air. The space heater clicked on. The fan whirring to life filled the silent room. Taking a deep breath, I let reality wash away the bad dream. I sat–arms wrapped around legs–until the bedroom warmed, my heart returned to its normal rhythm, and my shakes subsided. The peace from the previous night was shattered.

Intending to turn on the phone to see if Greg called or texted, I picked it up from its place on top of *The Frostlings*. That damned book again. First a hallucination, now a doozy of a nightmare. Maybe it was in the cellar for a reason. *Don't be stupid, it's only a book you're assigning too much meaning to.*

I chose not to stay in bed arguing with myself, forgot about the phone and swung my feet over the side to start my day. A lazy one of junk food gluttony and silly movies on my tablet sounded perfect.

After starting the coffee, I lit the fire, then stood with my back to it letting its warmth seep into my bones. The temperature plummeted. My breath curled into the air. No, no, no, not again. I turned–heart rolling then picking up speed–to the window expecting it to be open. It was not. The weak sunlight sparkled across the frost on the pane. The icy feathers twisted as if they beckoned me closer. *This isn't real. Just like yesterday wasn't real, like the dream wasn't.* Tippy-tap, tippy-tippy-tap sounded in the bedroom. A pause, then before I could decide whether to investigate or run from the cabin, they faded away. I crept to the bedroom to confront my hallucination while the temperature rose to normal.

The room appeared empty, but frosty footprints wound around the bed. On it my cell lay propped up on my pillow. *The Frostlings* sat beside the phone. Both seemed to leer from their positions of repose. I shuddered. Giggles in the living room. The darkened home screen brightened as a photo–oh god, not that one– flickered into place. I closed my eyes against it. Instead of the relief of darkness, the picture unfolded behind my eyelids. In it, Greg, my mother, and Kevin surrounded Maya while she blew out five candles on a birthday cake. The other patrons of the Horseshoe Bay restaurant–Maya's favorite–were a smear behind the wait staff looking at Maya and clapping. Kevin was wrong: I was to blame.

My fault. If I had stood up to my boss and left to be there for Maya's birthday dinner. If they hadn't stayed waiting for me after food and cake was done. If only the road hadn't been abnormally icy for Vancouver. Chimes and dings rang and rang. But none from Greg. Only wishes of condolences. Wishes of strength and love. Of pity for the woman whose family was wiped away on a curve while Greg yelled at me over speaker phone for not showing up. The last thing I heard before the terrible crush of metal?

My precious Maya giggling.

I remember hearing a tapping at the office window. Looking up, I saw a shape then a blossom of frost. I peeked at the frostlings that night and they took away my family. But now they gave them back along with my grief. Their twisted gift. Coming here to this frozen prairie of my youth was supposed to be a healing, a letting go. Instead, I'd kept up my illusion by texting a dead number and imagining he texted back, by listening to the voices of the dead on voicemail, including my own. For I was dead inside without them.

The curtain billowed from the breeze coming in the open window. The cold didn't touch me. Picking up my phone and *The Frostlings*, I crawled out the window and followed the little footprints in the snow heading through the field and to the woods. Giggles echoed around me.

My family waited.

Breathe

... Calvin D. Jim

The blizzard began at dusk as Cassie Li drove the lonely north Saskatchewan highway. The thrum of worn rubber wipers skipped across the windshield as lines of thick snow blew past her weather-beaten Toyota in a blur. Flowing waves of white obscured the road ahead and behind, leaving no trace she had ever travelled this way.

Cassie sighed. How could she have been so stupid? Driving out to the middle of nowhere to an address over two years old. He might not even be here anymore. Who would want to live in such a desolate place where it blizzards in mid-October? She glanced at the snow-covered aspen trees shadowing the thin strip of asphalt like crowds passing judgment, ready to throw her off the highway's steep shoulder dropping her into the deep ditch.

"Are we getting close now?"

Cassie glanced at her daughter Kayla, still strapped in her car seat in the rear, staring out the window, a tablet in her lap, the battery dead since Meadow Lake. She was probably hungry and her supply of granola bars and pretzels was dangerously low. This wasn't fair to her either. She should have left her with Joe. He would have taken good care of her and definitely would have fed her better.

She glanced at the fuel gauge. A quarter tank. They should have reached the town by now. She had to be lost. In this snowstorm, that would be easy.

"Not much further, Sweetie."

"Is that it?"

Cassie hunched forward and gazed through the windshield. Through the white-streaked darkness, a red neon sign loomed, a beacon in the storm. Wherever they were, it was still far from civilization, but there was some civilization here. She read the sign: Shanghai Moon Diner. A Chinese restaurant? Her heart beat fast. This might be it. He might be here after all.

Cassie slowed down and pulled the Toyota into a muddy parking lot and lurched toward the two-storey building. Patches of wood and insulation peeked through the dirty white stucco. The second floor looked like it had been tacked on as an afterthought, its walls still covered in black plastic tarp.

Cassie twisted the keys out of the ignition, opened the door, and exhaled a cloud of breath toward the night sky.

"Mommy, don't go in."

Cassie turned. "I'm right here, hun. I'll be right back."

She paced back and forth in front of the window, kicking at the fluffy snow, before spotting the glass door with faded black and gold letters glued to it that said "Chinese and Canadian cuisine." She tugged the handle, but it didn't budge. She glanced up and noticed the cardboard sign turned to "Closed."

Cassie swore under her breath. She hadn't come all this distance to be turned away.

She went to a window, wiped away some of the grime and gazed through it, looking for signs of life. The only light shone from the kitchen behind a serving window.

She stepped back from the window and stared up at the single second-storey window, lit in deep red through thin curtains. Someone was home. Someone lived and worked here.

"Hey, anyone home?"

She waited for a moment for someone to come to the window, but no one came.

Cassie turned her attention back to the glass door. She knocked, gently at first, then almost slamming her fist into the glass after only a few moments, her breath steaming up the glass. After what seemed like a long time, she saw movement. She wiped away the condensation and saw a woman dressed in a silken red Mao jacket and black slacks waddling toward the door holding a worn hardcover book.

The woman pointed to the sign. "Come back tomorrow."

Cassie waved frantically. "We're not here for food. I'm here to find someone."

But the woman waved her away. "No one here." She turned and waddled back toward the kitchen.

Cassie reached within her jacket and pulled out an old, soiled envelope and slammed it against the glass door, banging with the other hand on the glass. "My father. He sent this from here." She collapsed her head against the glass, steam from her breath clouding the window, warming her. "Please, I've come so far –"

The door quivered and the deadbolt unlocked.

Cassie started and gazed at the door as it opened. The woman reached out. "Let me see."

Cassie handed the woman the envelope. The woman gazed at it and nodded.

"Come, come," she said.

Cassie looked back at the car. "Just let me get my daughter."

"Daughter?"

Cassie ignored the woman's question, turned and retrieved Kayla from the car.

The woman brought Cassie and Kayla in and seated them at the counter on stools covered in cracked red faux-leather. She snapped on the light to the diner. A few fluorescent bulbs flickered on, the light only adding to the gloom. Some round tables covered in red tablecloths occupied the middle of a floor bordered by faux-leather-covered booths near the window and a long counter near the back. A cardboard "double happiness" sign written in gold Chinese characters hung on a wall between faded black-and-white pictures of unrecognizable cityscapes.

The woman walked behind the counter, opened the envelope, and started to read the old, cursive-written letter.

Cassie folded her arms. "Do you even know my father?"

The woman put the letter on the counter and nodded. "This was written long ago. How did you get it?"

Cassie gazed at Kayla, who had found a convenient plug-in and was now playing a math game on her tablet. "My mother passed away last year. I only found this and others like it a few weeks ago." She opened her purse and took out a bundle of elastic-bound envelopes.

The woman shuffled through the envelopes before gazing up at Cassie. "You have your mother's eyes."

"You knew her?"

"She is… was, my sister."

Cassie's mouth dropped and she stared at the woman. Sister? Her mother never mentioned a sister. The woman looked like Cassie's mother. But there was something different about her, something more confident and assured. Mother was never like that. She always seemed as depressed as her medication made her out to be. Why wouldn't she tell us she had family? Life could have been so much easier with family.

The woman bowed slightly and smiled. "I am Meiying."

"Uh, hi. I'm Cassie, and this little monster is Kayla." Cassie pulled Kayla close, almost pulling her off the round seat. "Say 'hello,' Kayla."

Kayla glanced at Meiying. "Hello."

Cassie turned back to Meiying. "Mother never mentioned you."

"She was a very independent type. But, not to worry, you're with family now."

"But she also had a few things to say about father –"

"Where are my manners. You two must be hungry." Meiying shuffled toward the kitchen. "I was just steaming some dumplings. Would you like some?"

Cassie nodded, her growling stomach reminding her that her last granola bar and coffee was hours ago. "Please don't go to much trouble."

Meiying waved her comment away. "Nonsense." She disappeared into the kitchen.

Cassie smiled and got up off the stool. She pulled out a cellular flip phone and pressed a number on auto-dial.

"Who are you calling, Mommy?"

Cassie raised a finger to her lips. "Joe. Shhh."

Kayla rolled her eyes. "Oh," she said before turning her gaze back to her game.

The phone wasn't connecting. Cassie gazed at it. No service.

"Damn." She shook the phone, raised the antenna, and moved around the restaurant, but the signal strength didn't increase. Text messages all came back undelivered. She was opening her email when Meiying appeared at the door carrying a covered tray. She snapped it shut and put the phone in her jacket pocket.

Meiying put the tray on the counter as Cassie rejoined Kayla. "I apologize for the spotty cellular service here. We have a regular landline if you need one."

Meiying lifted the cover. Steam billowed forth, revealing eight translucent dumplings in a steamer tray. Each dumpling had a flat bottom with a rounded bowl shape on top, ridges where each fold of the translucent rice dough was pinched to create a new fold.

"Soup dumplings," said Meiying, putting a small bowl of red vinegar near the tray of hot dumplings. "A specialty of mine from China. Be careful. They are hot."

Cassie grabbed a pair of chopsticks, picked up a soup dumpling, and bit into it. Almost instantly, hot soup dribbled down her chin. Kayla giggled and Cassie gave her a killer look as she leaned over her plate to let the soup dribble in.

"That is pretty," said Meiying, gazing at Cassie's chest.

Cassie looked down. A small black stone ring hung around her neck on a silver wheat chain necklace. It must have slipped out of her T-shirt when she dribbled her soup.

"It's black jade," said Cassie, composing herself with a napkin. "My mother gave it to me when I was ten."

Meiying reached toward the necklace but Cassie pulled back.

"May I?" Meiying asked.

"My mother said never to remove it."

"And have you ever?"

Cassie smiled, her eyes betraying the truth. "Well... she was very superstitious." Cassie reached behind her neck, undid the clasp and handed it to Meiying, who cradled the shiny black stone in her hand.

Cassie picked up another dumpling and hungrily wolfed it down, more carefully this time.

"Mommy?"

Cassie turned her gaze to Kayla, who was staring at the dumplings and backing away from the counter.

"Did you see that?" Kayla pointed at the dumplings with her chopsticks. "There's something in there. It hopped."

Cassie stared at the translucent dumplings. She could see a lump inside each of them and the brown of the broth, but nothing else. She hadn't shown any signs of being sick or feverish. She couldn't be. Was she seeing things? Cassie leaned in and touched Kayla's forehead.

Kayla moved away. "No, mom. There's really something in there."

In her peripheral vision, Cassie thought she saw something move. She turned and stared. It hopped inside the small shell. She couldn't tell the shape. She felt something in her stomach. Had she just eaten one of these? Bile rose in her throat and she gagged and covered her mouth. Shit. What had she eaten?

Cassie pointed at the dumplings. "What? What is in that?"

"You can feel it now, can't you?" said Meiying, not taking her eyes off the black jade necklace in her hand.

Cassie's head throbbed. Her vision blurred. It was hard to focus on her surroundings. The room began to spin and her body tingled. The nausea grew. She couldn't look away from the dumplings. Something moved within them. She could see them better now. Their body was thin, small tendrils came out from the body, snapping and stabbing at the translucent wall in front of them, trying to set themselves free.

Free to do what? And was one inside her?

Cassie felt a sharp pain stab at her. Her eyes widened and she doubled over and collapsed on the counter. She clenched her eyes shut.

Kayla ran to her mother's side. "Mommy. Mommy?!"

"Yes," said Meiying. "You can."

"What's in there?" said Kayla. "What did you feed us?!"

"She sees it too. That is good. Choice. He will like that."

Nausea welled up in her gut, threatening to explode. Cassie's heart pounded through her chest as she hyperventilated. Shaking, she pushed away from the counter, her knuckles white. She saw the kitchen door and bolted toward it, trying to keep the bile down. She ran through the doorway. Although the kitchen was to her left, there was a hall to her right and another door slightly ajar in front of her. From the cold draft coming from the cracks, it had to lead to the back of the restaurant.

Cassie burst through the door, collapsed onto the fresh blanket of snow and retched. The snow turned amber as her stomach sprayed the dumplings onto the ground. She coughed and spit and her chest heaved as her lungs fought to breathe.

Something dropped into the snow in front of her. She turned her gaze to the chestnut-coloured, wriggling, oblong form, no larger than her short fingernail. Was it a worm? A caterpillar? Neither of these would be alive this late in the year. No, the black dot on one end gave it away.

It was a maggot.

Cassie turned her gaze upward. Someone stood there in tattered black robes. And although he was mostly covered, his face was exposed. Maggots dug sores into the cheeks of his pale, gaunt face, exposing teeth and bone and dried blood. His eyes were sunken, pupils clouded over. The stench of rotting flesh made Cassie's stomach roil.

Cassie turned and scrambled backward into the doorway, heart racing.

"Cassie, dear," said Meiying through the screen. "This is Zhuyin. Your father."

Cassie screamed and blacked out.

Cold stabbed Cassie like icicles as she slowly regained consciousness. She pulled a scratchy wool blanket up around her shoulders as she shrunk into a shivering ball. A window rattled. A strong wind gust buffeted the fragile glass panes and threatened to shatter them.

Images stirred in Cassie's head. Unknowable things skittering beneath a dumpling's skin and inside her throat. A nightmare of flesh and bone and maggot.

Cassie propped herself up and a wave of nausea hit her. She winced, clenching her eyes shut. What had Meiying put in the dumplings? A drug? A sedative? Was what she witnessed real or illusion?

And where was Kayla?

Cassie snapped her eyes open. The small bedroom looked as if it were taken right out of the 1930s. She was on a rusty, iron-frame bed. Its sagging mattress squeaked with every movement. Rosewood dressers and chests of drawers, scratched and scuffed, flanked the bed. A matching vanity sat near the door. She gazed out the window. Outside lay many rusting hulks of cars and trucks, too many to count. Iron skeletons, their insides scooped out, left to die under the sky. Each one blanketed in snow, their only shroud in their final resting place.

"Kayla?"

Cassie swung her legs off the bed and sprinted toward the door. Without warning, something tugged at her ankle. She tripped and screamed as she fell to the slat wood floor.

Wincing in pain, Cassie propped herself back up and turned to find herself chained to the wall, cuffed in iron at her right ankle.

The floor creaked behind her. Cassie started and turned toward the bedroom door. Meiying stood in the doorway holding her wallet and identification. An aura surrounded her, pulsing and writhing with a yellowish, mesmerizing glow. A sudden hollow ache swelled in Cassie's gut like a wave, a desire lapping at the shore of her mind. Insatiable.

But not Kayla.

Cassie shook her head and clenched her eyes shut. When she opened them, Meiying's halo was still there. Cassie steeled herself. *Another side effect of the drug? It had to be.*

"Cassiopeia Li." Meiying huffed. "Arrogant mother, arrogant name."

Cassie bristled. Sure, in junior high Molly Wright and her clique teased her because of her "stuck-up" name. But soon she embraced it and loved her mother for choosing a name originating far, far from China.

Cassie stood up. "Where's my daughter? What do you want?"

Meiying shook her head and put Cassie's wallet on the vanity. "All in good time."

Something glinted around Meiying's neck, something familiar. Cassie's eyes widened and she reached for Meiying. "My necklace."

Meiying stepped back as if confronted by a rabid dog. "It was mine before your mother took it. It's a crutch, like your name. To prevent you from knowing where you came from."

Heat rose in Cassie's cheeks as she balled her hands into fists. Her mother gave her the black jade necklace; a gift, she said, from a long-lost uncle in China. "Mother was no thief."

"You're right." Meiying gazed into Cassie's eyes. "She was a monster."

Cassie leapt at her, clawing at Meiying, but the chain kept her from getting close. She collapsed on the floor. It was hopeless. Out in the middle of nowhere, no one knew where she was, not even Joe. There was no one for kilometres. And Kayla. She still hadn't answered where her daughter was. Was she chained up? Was she even alive? She should never have dragged her along. "We just want to go home. Let us go. We promise we won't bother you anymore."

"We're family. She is safe." Meiying crouched down. "Perhaps her grandfather can pay her a visit."

Cassie gulped. An image of the decaying husk standing in front of her flashed through her mind. She didn't want to think about the horrors it could visit on Kayla. But that wasn't her father. That thing was an illusion, a figment of her imagination brought on by whatever drug Meiying slipped into the dumplings. "He– he's not real."

"He *is* jiangshi, a Chinese vampire. You are his daughter and you have responsibilities." Meiying stood up, stroking the black jade neckless. "I will be back when you have calmed down and we can begin your lessons."

Meiying spun around and left. The creaky French door shut behind her as Cassie stared out at the window at the graveyard of cars.

Cassie sat in a booth in the darkened restaurant, staring out the window. Meiying had agreed to release Cassie. After all, Kayla was her chain. The blizzard hadn't let up and the wind shook the glass and whistled through cracks unseen.

Meiying sat down on the opposite side of the booth, still wearing the black jade necklace, and placed a small box covered in a cloth in front of her.

"Open it."

Cassie leaned forward and shook her head. "You said if I cooperate, you'd tell me where my daughter is. I'm here. Where is she?"

Meiying sat back against the cracked faux-leather seat. "You came here for money. Not your father."

Cassie felt heat rise in her cheeks.

"Your mother was never rich," Meiying said. "She struggled as I'm sure you do."

"How the fuck do you know?"

"She received letters, did she not?"

Cassie became lightheaded and she sat back. The letters she found seemed to arrive every few years no matter the address. Mother must have written back.

Meiying slid the box toward her. "In here, you will find all you need. You will want for nothing." She pulled the cover off the box. A small gopher lay in a rusted metal cage; a pulsing aquamarine aura emanated from its sleeping form.

Cassie gave her a blank look. "This is a joke. I want my daughter."

Meiying fiddled with the black jade pendant. "You are the daughter of a jiangshi. You have innate gifts–a birthright–your mother stole from you. Don't steal from *your* daughter." She caught her breath. "You have seen the aura, yes?"

Cassie nodded. Meiying's yellow aura still surrounded her.

"That is qi, the breath of life. Everything that breathes has one. Stronger aura, stronger breath."

Cassie gazed out at the snowstorm. What was Kayla's aura like? What color would it be? She turned back to the gopher. "So what's this about?"

"Use your gifts. Take its qi."

Cassie stiffened and a chill struck her gut as if she had just been tossed into a snowbank. This was a gift? If qi was the breath of life, taking it meant only one thing. "You want me to kill it?"

"It's a small animal. Its qi is weak, unrefined. You won't get much."

Cassie stared at the gopher and shook her head. "I–I can't. I won't –"

"Do you want to see your daughter again?"

Cassie clenched her jaw. Who was the monster now? She gazed down at the cracked faux leather seat. "F-fine."

"Lean in close and inhale deeply."

Cassie inhaled and as the musky odour of wet gopher, piss, and feces entered her nostrils, she grimaced and exhaled. "I'm getting nothing."

"Again."

Cassie rolled her eyes and inhaled. This time, a wisp of blue smoke rose from the gopher's snout toward her. The gopher twitched and whined as if it was having a bad dream, but it didn't move. "I–I can't –"

Meiying slammed her hand on the table, rattling the cutlery. "Continue."

Cassie inhaled again. The wisps of blue vapour entered her nostrils. Her heart beat faster as warmth flooded her chest and a tingling sensation travelled down her legs and her arms. She tilted her head back, letting it flop lazily from side to side, her eyes gazing toward the ceiling as if entranced, her mouth agape.

Images flooded her mind: tall fields of prickly grass; climbing high tree branches in the summer; tunneling through dirt and rock; bitter insects and moldy bread; the smell of iron during rain.

Cassie leaned forward and shook her head. What had she just experienced?

"The images…"

"Belonged to the creature. When you inhale their breath, you receive their essence."

Cassie gazed at the gopher. It was no longer twitching. Its jaw was open and its tiny torso wasn't moving. The aura was gone. It had taken its last breath.

Cassie covered her mouth. She had never killed anything before. She was shaking now, but the images, the elation. It washed over her like a warm, comforting wave. Meiying said everything in the box was all she would ever need. She was right.

"Do you want more?"

Cassie nodded hesitantly.

"When the restaurant opens, you can try again."

Cassie leaned back. "On a customer? A human?"

Meiying nodded.

A lightheadedness filled Cassie's brain. The idea of taking qi from someone excited her. What would she experience? How much of a rush would she get? But the cost. Taking qi from a rodent was one thing. But a person? Cassie shook her head. "I–I can't do that."

"Learn control." Meiying gritted her teeth. "Take only what you need."

Cassie gave her an incredulous look. "Why–why are you pushing me?"

"You have duties, responsibilities –"

"You keep saying that? What do you want me to do?"

"Give the qi you take to your father."

◇

There it was. The truth. At least part of it. Cassie sat back on the faux-leather seat.

"You are the only one who can give him the breath of life without risking death. He cannot go out as he is. He cannot even see unless it breathes. We waited too long before realizing your mother was never coming back and that she was with child."

Cassie stared out the window. "How long?"

"What do you mean?"

"How long before that walking corpse can pass as human?"

"Weeks, perhaps months."

Cassie shook her head. "No." She slid out from the booth. "I'm not your Energizer bunny."

Meiying gazed forward, toward the golden double happiness character on the other side of the restaurant. "Fine. You may go."

"What about my daughter? Where is she?"

Meiying turned her head slowly toward Cassie. "She stays."

"What?" Cassie smashed her fists into the table. The wooden laminate cracked and splintered.

Meiying flinched and slid toward the far end of the booth near the window, her eyes widened in a dazed stare.

Cassie looked at the table and back at her hands. Had she really done that? Didn't Meiying say qi would make her stronger? She could never have imagined this strong. She straightened herself. It was about time she had the upper hand.

"Kayla can see the breath of life like you," said Meiying. "Granddaughters of jiangshi don't normally inherit gifts, but sometimes it happens. If you won't take responsibility, then she will."

Cassie's mouth became a tight grimace. She smashed her fist into the table again. This time the table cracked and folded. "Take me to her. Now."

Meiying slid out of the booth. "Follow me." She strode toward the double doors that led into the kitchen and residence in the back, pushed them opened and disappeared behind them.

Cassie cursed to herself and began to run. She may be old, but she was wily. If she got too far ahead, Cassie may never catch her and she may vanish with Kayla.

The double doors opened and Meiying walked back in, hunting rifle in hand. She pointed it at her.

Cassie's eyes widened. She skidded to a halt and stumbled as she backed up and tried to turn around.

There was a loud bang and the acrid smell of gunpowder filled the air.

The bullet struck Cassie square in the stomach. She stumbled back, clutched her mid-section and collapsed on the floor, eyes, and mouth wide open. She stared at the ceiling, a coldness spreading through her body from the core. Or was that warmth? She couldn't tell anymore. She groaned as the pain throbbed from the wound, her breathing became ragged and uneven.

Footfalls drew closer. Meiying stood above her to her left, rifle pointed at her head. "No one threatens me, not even family."

Cassie opened her mouth to speak, but could only pant and taste copper in her mouth. Her lips, so dry. It took all her strength to lift her hand, now covered in blood. There was no recovering from this. She was too far gone.

"Your daughter will serve us well," said Meiying. "She is young and can be trained to respect her family, unlike you."

Cassie saw only one chance. She opened her mouth and rasped and with a bloody hand, she gestured for Meiying to come closer.

Meiying just shook her head and smiled. "I will not –
"

With her last ounce of strength, Cassie grabbed the barrel of the rifle.

Meiying pulled the trigger. The rifle fired, barely missing Cassie's head.

Cassie yanked on the rifle. Meiying collapsed on top of her and onto her open wound. Searing pain shot through Cassie like daggers. She screamed and clenched her eyes shut, concentrated, and inhaled.

Cassie pulled Meiying's breath of life into her. The warmth of qi enveloped her, spreading throughout her body from her core to the tips of her fingers. Cassie calmed herself, quieting her mind, concentrating on the strong flow of qi she received. Her skin tingled as calm turned into euphoria. She opened her eyes. Meiying seemed paralyzed. Her blank eyes stared into the void, her body as stiff as a corpse, even as Cassie inhaled her qi, draining her life.

And the images. A younger Meiying in a large city. Seawater, sweat and smog permeate the air. Hong Kong? Sadness as she discovers she is barren. Jealousy toward her younger sister for not being the same. Unwanted by her own family and tossed aside in favour of her younger sister. And Zhuyin, strong and handsome and powerful, hidden in a city of darkness. He promised her riches but needed a child first. A child she could not provide. All the others were gone. A father should never have to bury his children.

Cassie's eyes snapped open. "My mother. You should have protected her."

Meiying jerked backed to life and pulled away.

With her blood-soaked hand, Cassie grasped at the only thing within reach, the black jade necklace. She yanked hard. There was an audible snap as the necklace broke and Meiying collapsed on top of her. Cassie pushed her off and scrambled up. Meiying lay on her front, unmoving. Her aura was the colour of faded indigo. She was still alive. But a dark patch appeared near her neck, an area where the aura was not present. Meiying's neck was broken.

"Meiying?"

Cassie's bloody hand covered her mouth, still holding the black jade necklace. What has she done? She didn't mean to… But she was trying to kill her. Meiying would have forced Kayla into a life of slavery. Mother would have said all life is sacred, wouldn't she. It was for the better.

Cassie looked down at her blood-soaked shirt and lifted it up. There was no bullet hole. Not even a scratch. Qi. The breath of life saved her.

She looked back at Meiying. She couldn't just leave her alone. She had to help her. She turned Meiying's body onto her back. Her head flopped over at an unnatural angle, and her lifeless eyes stared into the void.

Cassie scrambled back into one of the stools by the counter, panting, almost hyperventilating. She never intended to harm Meiying, just take enough qi to heal herself and escape, not cripple her. Tears welled up in Cassie's eyes and she collapsed into wracking sobs.

She had become a monster.

The door near the kitchen opened. Someone or something was coming in from the blizzard.

Cassie wiped away tears and scrambled behind the end of the counter. She glanced around the corner into the service area and through the service window. The jiangshi hobbled into the restaurant.

Cassie pulled herself back, clutching her knees and closing her eyes, her whole body shaking. Would it notice her? Maybe if she could stop quivering so much.

The jiangshi snorted and snuffed, and Cassie peered around the corner. It was hunched over Meiying's body. It keened in a high-pitched screech.

Cassie pulled back and covered her ears. Was it sad? Did it know Meiying was still alive? She glanced around the corner again. The jiangshi inhaled loudly. Meiying's aura pulsed and faded as the last wisps of her breath of life were pulled in. Its face lost its mottled and decayed look. Muscle and bone cracked as it straightened up. It was healing itself.

And it was learning what happened here.

Cassie jumped up and ran. She ran past the jiangshi and slammed into the kitchen doors. Bits of Meiying's memories, mental detritus, flashed through her mind. She ran out the back door and into the blizzard. But she knew where Kayla was.

She ran between the piles of rusted and junked cars covered in blankets of thick snow and up the hill toward a small cabin. She opened the door. It was locked from the outside to prevent Kayla from leaving. The girl lay on an old couch wrapped in a tartan afghan, blanketed in an aura of bright orange. Embers glowed in the fireplace, but Kayla's aura shone brighter.

Cassie propped the door open to prevent it from closing and then walked to the couch. She leaned over Kayla's prone figure and then shook her gently to rouse her.

Kayla rubbed her eyes and gazed up at Cassie. "Mommy?"

"Kayla, hun."

Kayla sat up, hugged Cassie and buried her head into her chest. She trembled like a leaf and Cassie pulled her closer.

"I told you not to go inside," said Kayla.

"Time to go."

Kayla leaned back and nodded, furrowing her eyebrows.

Cassie knew that look. Kayla had seen the same horror as her. There may be many sleepless nights ahead.

Cassie and Kayla left the cabin and started down the hill. Suddenly, the jiangshi appeared from behind some of the junked vehicles. It strode up the hill toward them, no longer hobbling. Meiying's qi. It was her last gift, her last duty to him. It ran toward them.

There was no outrunning it. It would catch up to them long before she made it down the hill to her car. Cassie grabbed Kayla and slid into one of the cars and sat in the rusted metal seat, holding Kayla highly against her chest. What did Meiying say? It cannot see unless it breathes?

"Mommy," said Kayla.

Cassie put her fingers to her lips. "Shhh. Hold your breath."

Kayla opened her mouth to speak, but Cassie put a finger over her lips. "Don't breathe."

Kayla took a deep breath, and Cassie did the same. Only the wind and her heartbeat made any noise. Kayla's aura dimmed ever so slightly.

The horrid visage of dead flesh shambled into view, the jiangshi's laboured breathing growing louder as it drew closer.

Cassie gazed at its pockmarked face dripping with maggots. She strained not to exhale, to let the jiangshi know it was staring right at them with its lifeless, hollowed-out eyes.

She trembled as her heartbeat pounded through her chest like a sledgehammer. One breath was all it would take. One. Breath.

The jiangshi sniffed and leaned in toward her, tendrils of its cloying breath billowing over her, stinging her wide-open eyes. Then, it drew back, turned, and hobbled further up the path.

Cassie slowly let out a breath when she thought it was far enough away.

"Let's go, baby."

Kayla nodded and exhaled deeply.

They ran down the hill and around the restaurant and got into the car. A high-pitched scream came from up the hill. Maybe he had discovered Kayla was missing. Maybe he detected their breath and was coming after them. Cassie didn't care. They made it to her car and dove in. She started the car and backed out at full speed, windshield wipers clearing enough snow to let her see. Only when they had driven several kilometres did she get out and fully clear the windows.

When Cassie got back in the car, she took the blood-smeared necklace with the black jade pendant from her pocket, reached back and gave it to Kayla.

"It's a necklace. Put it on."

"It's got stuff on it."

"It doesn't matter. Put it on. We'll clean it later."

She glanced in the mirror as Kayla put the necklace on. "Thank you, Mommy."

Cassie drove down the lonely highway, waves of blowing snow crossing her path, the wind buffeting their car. She knew the euphoria of taking qi and the strength it provides. And she wanted more. And she could use that, couldn't she?

"Where are we going?"

"Home, pumpkin."

But there would be a few stops along the way.

Cassie breathed deeply. They would be fine.

Don't Count Your Chickens

... Stacey Kondla

Though the crescent moon was thin, it illuminated the farmyard and the creek in the valley below. The creature was easy to see as its white fur reflected the light of the moon. Ruth shrank behind the curtains in the kitchen window and held her breath. Her breathing and heartbeat roared in her ears, and the corner of the curtain grew moist in her hand. She could see it better than last time.

It moved across the driveway and stood under the shadow of the combine parked by the purple gas tank, a farm joke she loved. She could see its fur and the tall, yellow grass ruffle in the summer breeze. The field of wheat beyond sound like an ocean. The breeze tugged at the curtain in her hand. Peeping through the crack in the curtains, she could see the creature raise its muzzle to the breeze, pink nostrils flaring, yellow horns glinting in the moonlight, a soft snuffling sound coasting with the breeze through the open screen window. The sound caught her breath. She felt like her heart was jumping double-dutch in her chest. Her fist tightened on the damp curtain.

The creature sniffled toward the chicken coop that was down the hill from the house, its pugged muzzle pointing the way. It walked down the hill, on its two legs, upright like a person, but so definitely not a person. As it turned its back on the house and the little girl hiding behind the curtain, she began to shake, like you do after you throw up. She knew there would be fewer chickens to feed and water in the morning. Just like the last night when it was here.

Morning brought clouds and drizzle. A welcome relief from the heat of the past couple weeks and relief from the dust, too. The clay soil was slippery. Ruth was happy Dad had scattered fresh gravel on the path heading down the hill while the weather was good. Otherwise, she would have slid the whole way down. Otherwise, she might have seen its footprints. The gravel was loose and crunchy and solid to walk on. She liked the sound.

Unhooking the rusty hook-and-eye latch on the chicken coop door, she pushed into the food storage room. A cacophony of clucking and flapping came from the door opposite the one she entered. The fluttering caused a dust cloud to float and swirl around the room, eddies apparent in the light coming through the spaces in the boards. She latched the door closed again behind her and grabbed the dented, dusty bucket from beside the feed sacks. She dug the bucket in the feed, a puff of dust smelling of grass and earth found her nose. Sneezing and wiping her nose, she opened the chicken door and pushed into the coop to fill food trays and to count the chickens.

"We're missing more chickens, Mom," Ruth said as she poured milk into her oatmeal.

"Must be the coyotes again," sighed Mom. "I'll tell your father. He'll go hunting after work."

"Not coyotes. Also, there is no blood….."

"Don't start with that nonsense again, Ruth. It's tiring."

The fridge door slammed. And another sigh. Followed by a cupboard door slam and the clank of coffee mugs banging together.

"Mr. Johansson up the road left his family," Mom said. "Went out to outhouse and didn't come back in. Sharon is beside herself. You make sure you're nice to those Johansson kids at school next week."

Ruth felt a ball in her stomach. The Johansson's had been missing chickens, too, and their dog. She pushed her chair out from the table and away from her milky oatmeal. She left the kitchen quietly as her Mom bashed the pots around.

No school on Saturday and chores done meant Ruth had some time to herself and a pile homework to conquer before Monday. She sat at her tiny desk, pushed up against the window in the half story overlooking the farmyard. She pulled out her drawing pad and flipped to the page she had started last night. The creature stood under the moon, gazing up from the page, face in shadow, but she knew it was looking at her.

After supper, Mom and Dad sat out on the porch and talked about the chickens and Mr. Johansson. Ruth could hear their voices drifting up to her bedroom window. No breeze today. Just hot and dry, like Ruth's throat as she listened to Dad say he was going get that damn coyote tonight. The sun was setting as she watched Dad stomp across the drive to the barn where he kept his guns. She startled as she heard her bedroom door squeak open.

"You get to bed now. Those chickens need cleaning tomorrow."

"Alright, Mom," said Ruth. "I love you."

"Love you, too, Ruthie. Good night and sweet dreams."

Ruth crawled into bed, but left her curtains open. From her bed, she could see the moon. She loved the moon. No watching from the kitchen window tonight. Rolling on to her side, hugging a pillow close, Ruth felt sick in her stomach and more tired than ever before.

The next morning, Ruth was up and out of the house before her parents woke up. She shuffled down the gravelly path to the chicken house. Dad's shotgun was laying on the path in front of the chicken house door. She rubbed the goosebumps on her arms and swallowed hard to keep her stomach down where it belonged. Stepping over the gun, she opened the door of the chicken house, worrying about what she wasn't going to find in there.

When she got back into the house, Mom was in the kitchen fixing her coffee.

The rest of the day was bad. Mom on the phone frantically calling neighbors. Had anyone seen or heard from Stan? The shotgun was still on the path in front of the chicken house.

The evening left Ruth exhausted and her Mom with swollen, red eyes. Neither of them wanted to talk. There was nothing to say. Finally, Mom went to bed, closing the bedroom door behind her softly. The hair on the back of Ruth's neck stood up and she shivered as she made her way up the narrow, creaky stairwell to her room.

She put her hands on the top of her tiny desk and leaned over to look down on the drive and the rest of the farmyard. She could see the roof of the chicken house down the hill. She shivered as the wind blew dust devils around the yard and the tall grass by the barbwire fence leaned over. She closed the curtains. She couldn't look at the moon tonight. She didn't want to see what walked in the farmyard tonight.

Crawling under her blanket, Ruth cuddled her pillow tight. As tight as her heart felt in her chest. She felt like she was suffocating as her bedroom door squeaked open. She could smell cold. The hairs in her nose were stiff and she could barely breathe as the creature walked into her room and sniffled the air. The pattern from her curtains dappled its fur with orange paisley. And it looked straight at her. She gasped and the sudden rush of air sounded like an explosion in the silence.

In a blink, the creature was beside her bed and looked at her with ice blue eyes that looked like her Dad's.

Insatiable
... Marty Chan

Thomas Ritter gripped the reins, slowing his horse as he surveyed the mountain range on the horizon. Against the vast Alberta sky, the Rockies were a faint memory. His past belonged in the range's treacherous passes, where he oversaw the construction of the railroad tunnels. His future was firmly rooted in the ranch he had purchased from his earnings. He owned a luxurious home, several acres of land, and enough cattle to enjoy a comfortable life.

A pair of fawns loped toward a gully near the edge of his property. Decades of overflooding from the nearby river had carved it out, leaving watering holes for the deer and other animals in the area. Ritter snapped the reins and urged his horse toward the gully, scaring off the fawns. He stared at a mound of stones near the bottom. Under that pile, his present and his past converged.

He wheeled his steed around and galloped back up the hill. *Not today.* He needed to keep present and past apart. The cattle grazing on the slopes barely stirred as he breezed past them.

Ahead, he saw his home, his sanctuary. The roof peaks over the second-floor windows were the turrets of what Ritter's wife called their "cowboy castle." Lizzie and Mabel were playing on the veranda. Mabel heard their father's approach and practically vaulted off the porch to greet him. Her older sister, Lizzie, collected the dolls and placed them on the bench. Lizzie was the responsible one, taking after her father. Never one to leave things undone.

"Daddy!" Mabel yelled as she pawed at Ritter's stirrup. "I want to go for a ride. Take me!"

"Okay, sweetie."

He dismounted and hoisted his daughter on to his shoulders. She gripped his head and laughed as he walked his horse to the barn. Then he gripped Mabel's legs, let out a whinny, and pretended to gallop to the house.

"Let's see what your mother has made for dinner, shall we?"

"It's steak and beans. I helped."

"I'm sure it will be delicious, Mabel."

But eating was the last thing on Ritter's mind. At the dinner table, he absently pushed the food around his plate.

"For goodness sake," his wife said. "I swear you're worse than the girls. If you don't like what I cooked, just tell me."

Ritter looked up. "Sorry, Clara. It's good. I'm just not hungry. I'll eat it later."

"What's got into you, Thomas?"

"Nothing. Lost in my thoughts, I suppose."

"Would you like to unburden yourself?"

He forced a smile at his daughters. "No, you need to get these darlings to bed, and I have to catch up on some reading."

Clara raised an eyebrow as she took her husband's plate. "You reading? That's a first."

He rubbed Lizzie's blonde hair and kissed Mabel on the cheek. "You two get to bed now."

"Yes, Father," Lizzie said.

"I'm not sleepy," Mabel whined.

"Now," Clara said firmly. The girls scattered from the kitchen.

"I'll be in the study," Ritter said. "Just need a bit of time to clear my head."

"All right," Clara said.

Ritter headed down the hallway to his study, where he lit the lantern on the end table and nestled into his wingback chair. The fireplace crackled a few feet away, casting an orange glow across the room. He fished out a letter from his vest pocket, unfolded it, and read it again.

Dear Mr. Ritter,

I'm corresponding with you on behalf of Lu Sha-Kim, a Chinese priest who has come to Canada in search of the remains of Ji Wan-Shi. According to Mr. Lu, this man was a Chinese labourer in your employ during the construction of the Canadian Pacific Railway line through the Rocky Mountains.

It is our understanding that you were responsible for the burial arrangements of Ji Wan-Shi and may know the whereabouts of his grave. We would like to speak to you about the location of his remains. As per Chinese custom, his bones must be exhumed and returned to his village in China.

Lu Sha-Kim is prepared to pay a small sum in exchange for your information. Kindly respond to me at your earliest convenience.

Sincerely,
Robert Denton
Barrister

Ritter leaned back in his chair, reviewing the letter. The lantern flame danced from a draft in the room. Ritter glanced around, looking for what disturbed the air. Nothing. A crack came from behind. He jerked his head to look. Was it a log knot popping in the fireplace? No. Ritter had heard this sound before: the crack of rock from a pick being driven into it. He placed the letter on the end table, stood up, and paced around the room in search of the source of the noise.

A movement from outside the window. For a second, Ritter saw a dirty face in the glass. Was someone there? He peered closer. No sign of anyone. Behind him, a loud creak. He spun around, his fists clenched and ready for battle.

"Thomas?" Clara stood in the doorway. "What has gotten into you?"

Ritter lowered his fists. "Sorry. I guess I'm on edge."

She picked up the letter. "What's this?"

"Nothing to concern you."

She ignored him and skimmed the contents. "What is this about? They want to dig up a body?"

"It's nonsense. Pay it no mind."

"Do you even know this man they're talking about?"

Ritter shrugged. "It's some kind of misunderstanding. I wouldn't be able to tell one of those Chinese labourers from another. They all looked alike to me."

"Why would this priest think you arranged the funeral, then?"

"I'm not entirely sure, Clara. A lot of workers came and went on that project. I'm sure the priest got some wrong information."

"Well, it seems serious enough that he'd pay money to find the body."

"There's nothing I can do to help him," he said, taking the letter from his wife. "It's nothing to worry about."

"Are you certain?"

He smiled. "Put it out of your mind." He walked to the fireplace and tossed the letter into the flames. He watched as the fire consumed the paper, sending tendrils of smoke up the flume.

"It's morbid, if you ask me," Clara said. "Digging up bodies. Who would do that?"

Ritter kissed his wife on the cheek. "Go on. I'll come to bed shortly."

"Don't stay up too late."

"I will be right behind you."

Clara left the den. Silence descended on the room like a sheet over a corpse. Ritter stared at the letter turning to ash, his gaze fixed on the last of the message burning up. If only his past were as easy to erase.

Five weeks later, the heat of the Alberta summer bore down on the ranch. The previous night's thunderstorm had left huge puddles between the ranch house and the barn. The humid air weighed heavily on Ritter as he stacked bales of hay in his barn. The squalid heat turned his shirt into a wet rag that clung to every part of his skin.

"Excuse me, please. If I may have a moment," a man's voice called out from the barn entrance.

Ritter turned. A diminutive Chinese man dressed in a dusty black suit and spectacles stood ramrod straight in the doorway. The man's hair was cropped short, unlike the pigtails of the labourers who used to work for Ritter. The man extended a hand in greeting. No calluses. This man wasn't accustomed to an honest day's work, Ritter thought as he shook his hand.

"Good afternoon," the Chinese man spoke with a British accent. "My name is Lu Sha-Kim. You are Thomas Ritter, yes? Your wife said I would find you here."

Ritter let go. "Well, your search is over. What do you want?"

"Did you receive the letter my barrister sent?"

"Yeah. Can't help you. You wasted your time. I don't know about any dead workers."

"Sir, it is important that I locate the remains of Ji Wan-Shi."

"He's dead. I don't think he cares where he's buried."

"Not so, sir. His spirit will not rest until his bones are washed."

Ritter narrowed his gaze. "Come again?"

"It is a Chinese funeral... how would you say... custom? Ritual?"

"What of it?"

Lu explained, "Ten years after the body is buried, we must bring up the remains and wash the bones. Then the bones must be brought back to the Ji Wan-Shi's village so that his spirit can be reunited with his ancestors."

"Strange customs you Orientals have."

Lu bowed his head. "No different than yours. I might question why you would have a keepsake of a grandfather in your home or why you visit a mother's grave every year. The bones are important to Ji Wan-Shi's family. His spirit deserves a proper burial in his homeland."

"Well, to each his own. Like I said, I don't know anything about this man."

"I was informed otherwise. The workers who sent me here said you arranged for his burial in a local cemetery."

Ritter shrugged and turned to grab a hay bale. "Well, they told you wrong. I don't know where any Oriental is buried."

"Ji's friends said he died while he was working for you. You are certain you do not remember this man?"

"I hired a lot of your kind. Hard to keep track of who's who."

"He would have stood out. The workers claimed Ji Wan-Shi was a man who put their needs before his own. They said he was the one who represented them when they needed more rations. Apparently, wild animals tore into their supplies. He volunteered to discuss the matter with you."

Ritter set his bale on a pile, turned and shrugged. "Doesn't ring a bell."

"They told me you wouldn't give them more rations unless Ji agreed to plant the explosives in the mountain to blow open a tunnel. They said he didn't hesitate. He took the job."

"A lot of men took that job for the danger pay."

"They said something went wrong and the explosive went off before Ji Wan-Shi could get out of the tunnel. He was buried under the rubble. They said it took several days to recover his body."

"Accidents happened." Ritter's voice barely a whisper.

"They said they recognized his sacrifice and paid you to give him a proper burial out of respect for what he did for them."

"Sounds like a fabrication. The workers barely had money to pay for their rations. How could they pay to have an Oriental buried?"

"They said they gave up a month's pay in exchange for your promise to bury Ji Wan-Shi properly."

"They're mistaken. There's no way I could put an Oriental in a cemetery here. The locals wouldn't stand for it. We like to keep everyone separate, if you know what I mean." He turned and hoisted a hay bale.

Lu pushed the spectacles up the bridge of his nose. "I have no reason to believe they would lie to me."

Ritter slammed the hay bale down. "You accusing me of lying?"

The small man took a step back. "No, I would not say that. I'm merely trying to locate the bones of an honourable man. I was hoping you would be able to help me."

"Not my problem."

"This is urgent, sir. If Ji Wan-Shi's remains are not returned to his village and his ancestors, his spirit will not be able to rest."

"I don't know what to tell you," Ritter said, refusing to meet the man's gaze. "I had nothing to do with any dead Oriental."

Lu didn't budge. "I must find his bones. His spirit is disturbed. He will not rest until his bones are back with his ancestors. A spirit who cannot rest will wander the earth with one sole purpose."

"Why are you bothering anyway? I mean, it's just another labourer."

"Ji Wan-Shi came from a respected family. In China, he was a high-ranking soldier in the emperor's army. His family will pay handsomely if you are willing to help."

"I don't care about money. I just know that you can't bury an Oriental in a regular cemetery."

"I need to find the remains of Ji Wan-Shi. Please."

"I can't help you. You'll have to search on your own."

"Any information would be valuable and appreciated, sir."

Ritter wiped the sweat off his brow. "You want my advice? Don't bother with the cemeteries. I'd look for unmarked graves along the track."

"You won't help?"

Lu stared at Ritter. Their gazes locked in silence. Finally, Lu nodded and turned around to leave.

Ritter watched as the man mounted his horse and rode off past Clara, who had witnessed the entire exchange from outside. She stepped into the shadow of the barn, her eyes wide.

"Do you believe him about the spirit being disturbed, Thomas?"

He shook his head. "No, he's just trying to scare up some business, that's all."

"Why would he come all this way?"

"Who knows what those Orientals are thinking? I'll wager the labourers wanted the priest out of their hair and concocted a story about this burial. No way would I worry about one dead Oriental."

"What about his spirit? The priest said it would not rest," Clara said.

"Hogwash. There's no such thing as ghosts. He's one of those spiritualists, preying on people's grief so he can turn a dollar or two."

"I can imagine there are better ways to earn a living," she said.

"Either way, it's nothing that we should be worried about."

"What harm would it be if you just helped him look?" Clara asked.

Ritter took his wife by the hands and looked into her blue eyes. "We've got our hands full on the ranch, Clara. Trust me. It's a fool's errand that man's chasing."

She smiled and nodded. "All right." She wiped the sweat off her brow and left the barn.

Ritter returned to work, but as he grabbed the twine on the bale of hay, he stopped. He glanced over his shoulder at the stack of hay. He couldn't shake the feeling that someone was watching him, but he was alone in the barn.

He lowered the bale and stepped around the stack. A small pile of rocks sat on the ground. Ritter gritted his teeth at the tiny replica of the mound in the gully. He picked up one of the rocks and hurled it at the barn wall.

Mabel shrieked and jumped from behind a barrel, inches away from where the rock had struck the wall. "I'm sorry. I'm sorry."

Ritter rushed over to his daughter. "Are you all right?"

"I was just playing in the barn, daddy. I didn't mean to do anything wrong."

"It's not your fault. I didn't know you were there."

"I'm sorry, I'm sorry," Mabel said, her eyes moist with tears as she backed out of the barn.

"You did nothing wrong," Ritter called after her, but she turned and ran back to the house. Ritter sighed and shook his head. "Stupid Oriental got me all worked up," he muttered.

◊

The evening brought no respite from the oppressive and humid heat, nor did it allay Ritter's thoughts. The girls sat together in the wingback chair while he stared out the window at the approaching storm clouds. This was going to be a big one.

Crash! Ritter spun around, fearing the girls had knocked over a table. They sat on the big chair, happily reading. Neither of them seemed aware of the noise.

"Girls, did you hear that?"

His daughters looked up and smiled, puzzled. "What?" Lizzie asked.

"Sounded like the house was falling down."

They looked at each other before shaking their heads.

"You're not playing some kind of prank on me, are you?"

Lizzie shook her head. "No, Father. We heard nothing."

"Must have been thunder, I suppose." Ritter glanced out the window. No sign of lightning yet.

Mabel squeezed up against her sister. "I didn't do it, daddy."

"No, I'm not blaming you, sweetie," Ritter said. "Stay close to Lizzie."

He headed out of the study and into the hallway in search of the source of the sound. Clara was washing dishes in the kitchen.

"Did you drop something in here?" Ritter asked.

She turned around. "No. Why?"

"You didn't hear that crash? I swear the roof was falling down, it was so loud."

She shook her head. "Thomas, I heard nothing."

"You had to have heard it. I nearly jumped out of my boots."

"No, I didn't. Are you feeling all right?"

"Something fell, I know it." Ritter headed out the kitchen door. A chilling breeze greeted him as he stepped onto the porch. A cold front was blowing in, bringing with it some nasty clouds. Ritter's eyes stung from dust blowing into his face. He raised his arm as a shield while he looked for any damage to the exterior. The house was perfectly intact–not a board was loose. He circled the building a second time. Still no sign of damage, but it was hard to be sure in the dwindling light.

Ritter was about to go for a third time when Clara stepped out onto the porch. She wiped her hands on her apron. "Come in, Thomas. There was no noise."

"I swear I heard a crash," he called back.

"It must be the storm. Get in before the rain comes."

"One more look," he said. He walked to the corner of the house and stopped when he spotted the shadow of a figure in the study window. It was too tall to be one of the girls. He rushed to the front door, threw it open and charged inside.

"What are you doing here!?" he screamed as he skidded into the study.

Mabel and Lizzie jumped out of their seats. Mabel curled into a ball and began to cry. Lizzie hugged her sister and stared wide-eyed at their father.

Ritter paid them no attention as he rushed into the room in search of the figure he had seen in the window. "Where's the man?" he asked. "The one in the window."

Mabel sobbed while Lizzie shook her head. "We were the only ones here, Father."

Clara rushed into the study and hovered over the girls. "Have you lost your mind, Thomas?"

"I saw a man in the window. I'm sure of it. You saw him, Lizzie. You had to have seen him." He rushed from the window to his daughter, grabbing her by the arm and shaking it.

Lizzie cried, "Oh. No. That hurts, Father!"

"No one was here!" Mabel screamed.

"You had to have seen him," Ritter said. "He was right here."

Lizzie pulled away, nursing her arm. Mabel hugged her sister as they both shrank away from their father.

Clara waved her arm around the room. "Look. There's no one here now."

"Come out," Ritter ordered at the wall. "It has to be the priest from earlier. He sneaked into the house."

"Why would he do that, Thomas?"

"I don't know," he said. "I just know he's here. Come out!"

"Who is Father talking about?" Lizzie asked.

"Is there someone here?" Mabel cried.

"Shh, ssh. You're scaring the girls, Thomas."

"I'm telling you I saw a man in the window."

"The girls would have seen him."

"I swear I saw him. It has to have been the priest."

Clara pulled the girls to their feet. "Go to your room. Quick."

Ritter blocked the doorway. "No, it's not safe. He might be upstairs."

Mabel began to cry. Lizzie put her arm around her little sister's shoulder. Clara stood up. "Enough! Thomas. That's enough."

"I have to check the house."

"You do what you want, but I won't have you upsetting the girls anymore." Clara took both girls by the hands. "Come on. We're going to grandma's."

"But the storm is coming," Lizzie protested.

"He's here. I know I saw him," Ritter said.

Clara yanked the girls away and backed out the doorway. "Don't follow us!" she said, glaring at her husband as she wrapped her protective arms around her daughters.

Ritter stepped back as his family left the study. He could hear their voices receding in the hallway: Mabel asking, "What's wrong with Daddy?" Clara saying, "I don't know, honey. We'll be okay. Let's go." Lizzie protesting, "But the storm." And, finally, Clara: "If we move quickly, we should be able to beat it. Hurry. Out, out."

The front door slammed shut, leaving Ritter alone in the study, but he was sure he was not alone. He would apologize later for upsetting his wife and daughters, but right now he had to deal with the intruder in his house. Ritter grabbed the rifle from over the fireplace and headed into the hallway. He was positive the priest was behind all of this and was lurking somewhere in the house.

The rooms on the main floor were empty. No sign of anyone. Ritter eyed the stairs leading up to the second-floor bedrooms. He swung his rifle around to aim up the stairwell.

"I'm coming up. This is your last chance to come out."

No answer.

He began to climb the stairs. They creaked under his feet as he ascended. No time for stealth. He had the rifle, and he wouldn't hesitate to pull the trigger if needed. At the top of the stairs, Ritter raised his weapon and inched toward the first door. He kicked it open and swung the rifle into the room. Empty.

He closed the door and checked his daughters' room. Again, nothing. That left his bedroom. He crept to the end of the hallway, his palms moist and his heart pounding. He shouldered the door open and jumped inside.

On the neatly made bed sat a rock. Ritter lowered his rifle and walked over to the bed to pick up the rock. He gritted his teeth and shouted, "I know you're here! I have a gun. You had better clear out before I use it."

No answer.

Ritter headed out of the bedroom and down the hallway. He stopped at the top of the stairs. Below, another rock sat on the wooden floor, as if it were marking a trail for Ritter to follow. He ran down the stairs.

"Get out of my house!"

A loud rumble in the distance answered him. Thunder was announcing the coming of the rainstorm.

Other than the rock on the floor, there was no sign of the priest. He had either found a perfect hiding place, or he had left the house.

"Come out!" Ritter ordered once more.

He entered the study. "Leave us alone. I don't know anything about the dead Oriental."

Something or someone began pounding against the wall. Not just one wall. All the walls. It sounded like a hundred pickaxes smashing rocks. Ritter covered his ears, but the sound pierced his hands and drove straight into his mind.

The sound would not relent. Ritter swung the rifle at one of the walls and fired into it, hoping to scare off the intruder. The noise stopped.

He inched to the window to peer outside. The first drops of rain streaked the glass. No sign of anyone out there.

"I did nothing wrong!" he howled at the darkness outside.

The rain pelted the house. The storm had arrived.

Ritter knew what he had to do. He headed out of the house. The cold wind blew against his face as droplets of rain splashed across his face. He surged ahead to the barn.

Inside he saddled his horse and grabbed a shovel. He mounted his steed and rode out into the dark night. Overhead, the pregnant storm clouds unleashed a torrent of rain. Flashes of lightning lit up the hills. Ritter urged the horse toward the gully.

The rain pelted his face as he leaned forward to protect himself from the elements. The horse galloped as the wind whipped at Ritter's drenched clothes. He clutched the reins and stared ahead.

Finally, he reached the gully. He climbed off the horse and grabbed the shovel. A clap of thunder spooked the horse away. The storm was directly overhead.

Ritter navigated the pooling water to the mound of stones. He stabbed the shovel into the dirt and started clearing the rocks, tossing them into a heap next to him. When he'd made short work of the heap, he picked up the shovel and began to dig.

The blade of the shovel bit into the softened soil. Ritter hoisted up hug clumps of dirt and tossed them over his shoulder. The water filled up the hole he had been digging, but he had no way to stop.

Each time he drove the shovel into the mud, his mind raced with terrible images of the dead. His teeth chattered as the rain drenched him. Though he wanted to run away and be with his wife and children, he knew the only way to end this was down. The mud sucked him down to his knees. Frantic, he continued to dig. His arms ached after what seemed like hours. As he dug, a rancid stench from beneath rose and burrowed up Ritter's nose. He winced at the foul odour.

"Where are you? Come on. I know you're here," Ritter muttered as he slung spade after spade of wet soil.

The skies lit up and released even more rain. The river started to overflow. Water poured into the grave. He redoubled his efforts to clear both dirt and water from the hole. His shovel blade hit something soft and suddenly the mud gave way, dropping Ritter two feet down into a mess of collapsing haybales and loose dirt. He had forgotten about the bales he had used to fill the hole. River water now flooded over him.

It was pointless to continue. He had to get out. He gripped the edge of the hole and tried to climb out, but the mud broke away in clumps. He fell back in.

"Damn you!" he shouted. He used the shovel to prop himself up but he was stuck in the muck. The shovel sunk into the wet dirt as more water poured down on him.

His hand finally grabbed onto an edge that didn't crumble. He began to pull himself out, but something took hold of his pant leg. He tried to pull himself out, but the grip was firm. He clawed wildly, searching for more ground to grab and haul himself clear. The hole was flooding up to his neck now.

He slipped under the water. His arms thrashed until his head broke the surface. He gasped for air, but he couldn't shake free from whatever was clutching his leg. Another fresh deluge roared over the edge of the hole.

Ritter went under a second time. His chest tightened, but he couldn't tell if it was from the exertion or dread. He flailed in the mud. He tried to stretch up for another gulp of air, but now the water level was well over his head. He wanted to rip off the wet clothes that wrapped around him like a shroud.

With a desperate lunge, he broke the surface of the water. He grabbed the side of the hole, gasping for air. He reached out and grabbed at the pile of rocks he had discarded to the side. He wanted to beg for mercy, but words died in his throat. With one last push, he reached for the pile. The heap tumbled over, and stones rolled toward him. A large one glanced off his forehead as it fell into the water.

Stunned, he sank as more water poured over him and filled his mouth and nose. His hands clawed helplessly at the air. The water burned his throat and nose and filled his lungs. The memories of his sins flooded his panicked mind. He thrashed, unable to reach the surface again. He opened his mouth, and the filthy water filled his lungs. He couldn't breathe. He couldn't rise. He couldn't...

His body convulsed once more, then went still. He could feel himself slipping away into the darkness. His eyes bulged open, but he could no longer see. The grave he had dug now claimed him. He was gone. The rain subsided.

Ritter's lifeless body floated to the surface, finally free of whatever held him down. His still form bobbed in the flooded hole. Around him, a skeleton hand bobbed to the surface, a torn piece of his pants in its fingers. Another human bone popped to the surface. And another. The remains of Ji Wan-Shi now floated around the corpse of Thomas Ritter.

The water had washed the bones clean.

Arsenic and Old Men

... Taija Morgan

Fall 1950

John Toppan was four years old when a witch spat in his
father's eye and cursed their family for swindling her out
of vast golden fields of farmland. "There's poison in yer
blood, mister," she'd said as John peeked out from
behind Ma's apron. "Call *me* a witch? Here's a curse for
the lot of ye: every Toppan shall die at a Toppan's hand,
his own or his kin's. Ye bring yer suffering on
yerselves." John's older brother William hadn't been
there to hear the witch's words, and to this day he didn't
believe them, but they'd always come to pass.

John was seventy now, and with only the two Toppan
brothers left to bear the weight of the family name, he
couldn't help suspecting how their cursed fates would
come to pass. The sun-kissed prairie land withered under
his father's care, long since barren. Retirement from his
beloved pharmacy kept John confined and atrophied in
this ancient house. The windswept fields beyond the
curtained windows were no balm to his soul. He had
nothing but time to speculate on the role his brother
would play in his demise.

William peered over his glasses, setting his newspaper on their breakfast table. "Retirement's not all bad," William said, the lie slipping past his lips with the ease of repetition. "Take up needlework, like Ma— women's work was always better suited to you. Nothing too strenuous, lest you get your heart going." He poured himself some tea, black. "Take care of yourself while I'm away, Johnny. Wouldn't want anything *happening* to you. You know how I worry about my little brother."

John narrowed his eyes. "Of course. Wouldn't want an accident, would we? I'm sure you'd be beside yourself."

William stared, unreadable. "Get plenty of rest. It'll do you good."

There it was. Rest. That must be part of his scheme. John didn't know the specifics, but William had something planned to get rid of him. They'd been at each other's throats for a month since John's forced retirement after his heart attack. Longer, if one counted the seventy years of sibling rivalry, which John did. "You'd like that, wouldn't you?"

"Might put you in a better mood, brother dear." William slurped at the lip of his Paris-green teacup, lifting the paper.

Slurp. Slurp. Slurp.

Skitter.

John's breath caught at the distinctive sound. He slapped his hand on the table and tilted his head. His gaze slid toward the source: the cellar door. "There! Did you hear it?" The scurrying, the scratching. It was unmistakable. John shivered. If the cellar was compromised, it would destroy their emergency food stores for the winter. If they got snowed in way out here in the prairies without their supplies and the nearest neighbour miles away... *catastrophe.* Was this William's doing?

William lowered the paper an inch. A drop of tea collected at the tip of his moustache and lingered, trembling, but didn't fall. The kitchen was silent. "I don't hear anything."

Drip. Splat.

"I'm telling you, there are mice in the cellar."

William huffed, glaring. "Paranoia is not a becoming trait, Johnny."

John clenched a fist against his knee. "I heard them."

"And I did *not*." William slammed his teacup onto its saucer. A porcelain chip flew across the table. "If there *are* mice, I'll take care of them. You never mind. I'll be cross if I return to find you've brought any foul chemicals into this home, you know I will."

John looked away. "You're always cross."

"I mean it." William returned to his paper, ignoring the drop of tea now staring at them from the polished tabletop. A faint *titch-titch-scritch* echoed from the locked cellar. William was going deaf in his old age. Or, he planned this. Was that even possible? Could William have unleashed mice in the house just to torment John? To make him ill? It would risk his own health too, his own food stores.

He ground his teeth. Filthy things. William was unconcerned *or* a conspirator. If he wasn't conspiring with the mice, what would William do about them that

John couldn't? William knew mousetraps were useless without poison. These mice would laugh at them outright. It had been more than half a century since the unfortunate incident with the rat poison–surely they could move past it by now.

William hacked into his handkerchief. "Honora will be by to clean today–don't forget to pay the girl. Are you certain you'll be all right here without a vehicle while I'm gone?"

"I'll survive. Have a pleasant time, brother."

As soon as William left, John grabbed his cane. He ambled around in search of something to use against the rodent invaders. He was certain they must have some rodent poison secreted away. A chill had pierced the air this last week, warning of the change of season upon them. John shuddered as he worked his way through the empty house, listening to the discordant serenade of the mice.

Spring 1888 | Age 8

A sharp line divided the light of the kitchen from the fearsome dark of the cellar. Cold crawled up the steps, wrapping invisible fingers around John's bare ankles. He shivered.

"Put this in the cellar for those filthy mice, Johnny. We'll soon get rid of them." Ma cupped his cheek with a warm palm and smiled before smoothing out her apron. Purple flowers adorned its edges–belladonnas, like the ones in her special garden. The house smelled of fresh apple pie and so did she. But the cellar...there was always an awful smell down there.

John stood at the open door. He had bait, traps, and a tin in hand–and strict instructions on how to use it. He was a big boy and Ma trusted him even if no one else did. She'd taught him about every herb in the garden, every medicine in the cabinet, and now every poison on the property. Ma had shared her passion for botany and chemistry, and her respect for nature.

He would make her proud. This was a small task. A delivery, of sorts.

John thought of the boys last summer poking sticks at a large dead mouse in a neighbour's barn, its stiff body, limbs curled up in agony, lips pulled back over gnashing teeth as if it had been trying to scream in its final moments as a human might. Its eyes had been empty holes, scooped right out.

His stomach dropped. John had vomited into a pile of straw and the boys teased him until William socked one of them in the mouth.

Ma said the mice would eat all their food and they'd starve or get sick, so they had to protect the family. Protecting the family was everything. That's what Ma did when men came by asking for money when they couldn't pay a bill and Father was away a long time for work–she made them go away, made them stop asking questions, protected the family. It was a special secret she and John kept from Father and even William, because sometimes keeping secrets meant keeping people safe.

Now, John had to protect them in a different way. He wasn't killing the mice himself, he was setting the poison out and they were killing themselves, Ma said. He was not a murderer. Well, he *was*...but he *wasn't*.

He was a Toppan, though. He knew about the curse. There was something bad in John; the witch said so. His father hurt people, especially his family. His uncles had seen the witch and then killed each other. There were lots of bad, dead Toppans now. John didn't feel like he was bad, and William said folks in the nearby hamlet of Noddington were wrong to call them cursed, but John didn't see a way around it. Those he loved would surely kill him, or he would kill them first.

Ma glanced at him. "Well, go on."

John shook his head. His feet wouldn't move. His heart raced, and he took a deep breath. "It's too dark."

"Take a lamp then, silly lamb." She nodded to the lamp on a ledge. She reached for a box of matches. When she stood over him in the threshold, the warmth of her kept the chill at bay.

He leaned into her, wanting to ask if poisoning the mice was murder and would God think so too, but he knew it was silly to wonder. They were only mice. Father would smack him for asking, call him weak.

His hand pressed against his chest. A horse galloped beneath his ribcage. "Why's it so dark down there when it's so bright up here, Ma?" he said instead, just to have something to talk about. Her shadow blurred the hard line of light on the floor as she moved, her dress swishing.

"Well," she considered seriously as she usually did when he asked her serious questions, "the dark needs to go somewhere in the daytime. When we're awake, it goes deep down, until nighttime when we're asleep. Then it comes back out." She struck the match, scaring the darkness away like scattering mice.

"But it's always there, even when we can't see it? Just waiting?"

"I suppose." She nudged him down the steps. "Now go on."

Flickering light in one hand, poison in the other, John stepped into the darkness.

Fall 1950

By evening, John had made no progress dealing with the mice. He sat on the porch for a while, staring out at the bald, flat earth until the harsh winds forced him back inside. The maid delivered some pie on her visit, which lifted his mood. If William had left him the vehicle, he'd have gone into Noddington and picked up some rodent poison. But with his old bones as rickety as they were these days, John was confined to the property. He regretted not asking Honora for a favour, but it would get back to his brother if he did.

He'd found many half-empty blue bottles of paregoric in the cupboards, the "camphorated tincture of opium" labels long faded though John didn't need labels after a lifetime in the pharmacy. They used the mixture often as an effective cure-all for anything from pain to diarrhea to a bad cough. William's brandy also lined the shelves, and plenty of ointments, but no rodent poison. William refused to allow it on the property.

John paced in the kitchen, wearing a hole through his slipper. His knee ached, but he didn't stop. He heard them. They were everywhere. If he found them, he'd –

Skitter. Skitter. Skitter.

Squeak.

There!

Fists clenched, he froze in place, head tilted, eyes bright and alert. A sharp, unmistakable mouse squeak. He wasn't going mad.

Turning toward the source of the noise, John glared at the cellar door. He unlocked it and swung it open with a bang, startling himself. The mice silenced.

He'd checked the cellar first. No mice, no poisons. But that was during the daylight. Things looked different at night. Perhaps he hadn't been thorough. He stared down into the darkness of the cellar below but found his limbs stiff as though gripped in ice.

Heart working its way into a sluggish gallop, John lifted his hand to his chest and frowned.

Then a laugh swelled up in his throat and spilled out. Such childishness in his old age!

Take a lamp then, silly lamb, he thought to himself, grabbing for the lamp on the table and heading deep down into the dark to rid the house of these nasty vermin once and for all.

There it was in a cobwebbed corner. The rusted tin declared: ARSENIC.

◊

After John laid the poison out, the house was quiet. Whatever William had planned to trick John into injury– or worse–in his absence hadn't come to pass, though John searched and avoided potential traps. When he slept, it was restful. Then his brother returned, and it was as if the mice sensed they were at liberty to resume their conquest.

William's voice boomed from the kitchen. "Where did this come from?"

John froze in the drawing room, a pipe dangling from his lips.

When his brother stomped in, red-faced, the last words John expected were "Apple pie? You brought apple pie into this house?"

John sputtered. "I–I didn't. Honora brought it when she came to clean."

William hacked into his handkerchief before pointing a finger. "You *know* I hate apple pie."

"It's only pie. You're being unreasonable."

William's fists clenched at his sides. John stared. In fits such as these, John was certain William would strike him down and kill him where he stood. He looked just like their father in these moments, and John often wondered if he realized it and if that was the only thing stopping him–the cold fear of being like the man they'd both grown up hating.

Without another word, William stormed out, clanked around in the kitchen, and slammed a few doors before settling down.

Hours later William was puttering in the living room, humming Beethoven's fifth symphony under his breath–off-key, hacking up phlegm the whole time–allayed of his rage now that he had disposed of the offensive pie.

John remembered the camphorated tincture of opium in the blue bottles he'd found earlier. A bit of medicine, John's special mixture, would do the trick on William's no-doubt-sore throat and tumultuous mood. Perhaps prevent him from conspiring for the next day or so. It would do his brother good to rest, as William so wanted John to.

John slipped into the kitchen. A hearty dose of paregoric in William's brandy and a touch of arsenic would combine perfectly to cure any ails. As Paracelsus said, it was only the dose that made the poison. Harmless, in competent hands. He had been a pharmacist for decades, and there were no more competent hands than his.

He waited for William to hack into his handkerchief, then emerged with a tumbler. "Your throat sounds dreadful, dear brother. Must be getting sick. I made you my specialty–can't even taste the medicine."

William glanced down at the glass. "I feel fine."

"Your voice is raspy, and that cough. I don't doubt you caught ill on your fishing trip. Best to address it before it takes hold."

"Hmm, well, I suppose." William did enjoy his brandy. The paregoric, he didn't mind, though John may have overdone it–the brandy would cover the taste. The arsenic…well, he didn't need to know about that.

William took the tumbler and drank. "Thoughtful of you," he added with a note of suspicion.

John shrugged and smiled. "You're always taking such good care of me."

Can't say I'm feeling quite myself," William said at dinner the next night, one hand worrying at his belt buckle while the other pushed food around his plate. "Perhaps the fishing trip took it out of me." He declared this as a personal revelation, as though John hadn't suggested it.

"I'm told there's a bad bout of stomach sickness making the rounds," John said. "Nothing to fret about, so long as it's treated."

William wheezed into his handkerchief. "Told? By whom? You never leave the house. You haven't any friends."

"Mr. Scheele said a slew of parishioners are ill."

William scowled. "The milkman? He's a fool, I wouldn't take his word for anything." He wiped fevered perspiration from his forehead.

"Are you all right?" John placed a hand on William's shoulder. "You look pale."

William pushed his plate away. John set out a double shot of his special solution for William later that night, pleased when thirty minutes later the house was once again peaceful and silent. Even the mice slept through the night.

◊

John always imagined his parents' first meeting as something out of a storybook. Ma said their eyes met across a field of golden wheat–Father in a travel-wrinkled suit, Ma in a flowing white dress–and theirs was love at first sight.

"That's *not* the story," William said. "Your memory is about as effective at capturing nuance as a sieve is at capturing water." William chuckled at his joke, then groaned and clutched his stomach. Velvet curtains blocked out the sunlight and the silent prairies beyond the window, obscuring the vine-patterned green-and-copper wallpaper inside.

"I don't know what you mean," John said from his bedside. The wallpaper peeled at the corners. This old house was falling apart but they'd never changed it–it looked just as it did when their parents were alive more than a half century ago. John wondered if they'd ever leave this place, this poison witch-land. The endless barren fields and lashing winds. He hated it here. He hated that he loved it, even more so.

"You never noticed Father's wandering eye? Or Ma's gentleman friends frequenting the house when Father was on the road?"

John balked. "Ma had no gentleman friends. That you would even entertain such a thought is more a reflection on your character than on her sainted memory."

"Ah, you were young then. You wouldn't have noticed." William slurped his tea.

Slurp. Slurp. Slurp.

Behind the green wallpaper, the mice worked in the walls.

Skitter. Skitter. Skitter.

"You forget I'm only three years younger, dear brother." John glared at William in the dark.

"And infinitely more naïve." He laughed, as though fouling the memory of their mother was great entertainment for him. "Mr. Gilman–why, that was such a scandal, the poor bloke skipped town for good."

John stilled. "You mean…the tax man?" He turned to look at his brother.

"Yes, that's the one."

John shook his head. "That wasn't–Ma, she was taking care of us. The family. You…you didn't know her like I did back then. You weren't there, you were always off with Father. It wasn't like you think."

William's brows knitted together. He leaned forward. "What on earth are you going on about?"

John glanced over at Ma's painting on the wall. She watched, listened. He thought of the cellar. No, they could never leave this land. "Never mind. Forget I brought it up. How's your stomach today?"

John administered more of his special medicine–a little extra–and any unpleasant conversations fell asleep with William. A sense of peace and control blanketed John as his brother slept, knowing that in the land of dreams no dark machinations were working against him–with William under his watchful eye, John was safe, the house quiet.

But never for long. His brother had always been his most difficult patient when he took ill.

"Would you bring me some *fresh* tea, Johnny?" he'd demanded the next morning. "Hot, this time, if you will–I'm so cold. You know how the kettle works, don't you?"

And at lunch: "My God, this broth is terrible. I'd sooner starve."

"Oh, my aching bones," he whined all evening. "And my *stomach*–I cannot stand this pain! I'm getting worse. Perhaps we should send for the doctor?"

John had suffered long enough. "Nonsense," John spat. "Haven't I always taken care of you when you are ill?"

William perked up at having elicited John's irritation. "Dear brother, you are not a doctor. You *were* a pharmacist and now you're not. Forgive me if I'd like a *professional* opinion."

Such a jibe was vicious, even for William. John ground his teeth until his jaw ached. He ignored the request. The mice too were growing bolder. As John gathered up a tray, he glimpsed a tail slithering into the shadows.

He checked the traps he'd laid out only to find he hadn't killed a single mouse. He doubled his efforts.

John set a tray of bland food on his brother's bedside table a few days later. He peeked out the window–no snow yet, but the grey skies threatened. The lonesome fields shimmered in the dim overcast light, stiff with a thin crust of frost.

"Johnny?"

"Yes? More tea?"

"No, I was just thinking." William pulled his blankets to his chin and turned to look at John in the armchair. "Do you remember winter skating on the lake?"

"I remember many such winters."

"The time we built those ice castles? Remember how many hours we spent, cold to the bone, fashioning our snow kingdom?" William looked like a young boy then, all wrapped up in tattersall quilts.

John smirked. "I remember."

"I don't think I've ever had as much fun as I did then. The other boys wouldn't come out to play."

"Their mothers wouldn't let them. Ours was dead. Father wasn't around much then." John frowned.

"We were like two renegades. It's a wonder we survived! Remember the stew I would make us? The same one every night for weeks. I thought you'd go on a hunger strike."

John's lip curled at the memory. "Ugh, yes, horrible."

William chuckled, his face soft with good humour. "We ate like kings when summer rolled around."

"When did Father return that year?"

"Oh, not for a few months. It was when Aunt Ethyl didn't show up to watch us. Father was so angry. But we managed on our own. Quite the pair of scamps back then, finding trouble."

John smiled. "I seem to recall finding more of that trouble than you did."

"Well, I was the oldest. Someone had to look out for you. Oh my, do you recall the incident skating on the ice that winter?" William wheezed into his handkerchief.

"How could I forget?" John leaned back. "You were furious."

A memory fluttered past the edges of his thoughts: water like shards of glass in his young lungs and the haunting whisper of his dead mother's voice beneath the shock-cold ice, mouthing in his ear like a dream, *My little lamb, it's so cold down here. Let's go home.* William's hand reaching out, grabbing, pulling him back to the surface. John shook his head and the memory washed away.

William was quiet for a long moment and John wondered if he had fallen asleep.

"Scared the devil out of me," William murmured into his quilts. "Almost lost you."

"Pulled me out by my bootstraps." John smirked. "Then you made us hot cocoa, remember? You never tattled on me to Father."

William didn't answer. John looked over at him. His eyes were closed.

"William?"

Silence.

John's heart stuttered in his ribcage as he waited, waited, *waited* for William's chest to rise with air. When it did, John breathed out a long sigh, surprised to find himself relieved. Perhaps he was making a mistake, he realized, toying with his brother's life. William was all he had left in the world, and here he was, slipping poison into a drink.

John had done this before to disastrous results, and William had been the one to cover for him, back him up, support him–William had always been his brother's keeper. How did he let this go on so long?

John needed to stop. He would stop. Obsessing over a witch's curse was childish. This was the end. John returned the arsenic to a shelf in the cellar and locked the door.

Summer 1890 | Age 10

Protecting the family was everything, his parents always told him. Until it wasn't. Ten-year-old John had been wrapped in dreams and a soft quilt when Ma's voice stirred him awake.

"Come, little lambs. I have a surprise."

He pawed at sleep-crusted eyes and squinted into a glowing lamp.

"Ma?" William asked from the bed next to his.

"We're going on an adventure!" Her smile pulled so tight it looked ready to snap. A crown of purple flowers adorned her head. He wouldn't notice the red puffiness of her eyes until he looked back on that night much later. "Just us, under the stars. A picnic with apple pie and milk. What do you say?"

John wished he could return to that moment. He'd say, What's wrong, Ma? Talk to us, we'll sort it. He'd say, Come to bed, everything will look different in the morning–you'll see.

But he was a child, and he had yet to put away his childish thoughts, so John had his shoes on as soon as she mentioned apple pie. Ma laughed like a ringing bell and his chest filled with sunshine in the darkness. She handed John the picnic basket and entrusted William with the light.

John skipped after her. His brother followed at a more cautious pace. William eyed their mother as they trekked away from the house through the fields of golden wheat and out toward the lake. Ma sang lullabies–bible verses, hymns, and poems. She sang anything and called it a lullaby. The lamp lit their way, but they hardly needed it with the blanket of stars and the moon full-to-bursting above them.

When the house was out of sight, John remembered their father had been home when they'd gone to sleep. "Where's Father?"

Ma picked up her pace. "He's gone. He's left us. But don't worry, little lambs, we don't need him anymore. We'll soon be free as the stars." She spread her arms wide as if she could pluck them right out of the sky.

John stumbled. "Is he coming back?"

She halted. "No."

They stopped. She turned to stare at them, her chin tipped toward the moon.

Tears swelled in his throat, but William's warm hand landed on his shoulder and squeezed enough to hurt. John glanced at his brother in the half-dark and saw him shake his head without moving it, cold seriousness on his face.

Brows furrowed, he looked at Ma, took in the bright wildness in her eyes he'd never seen directed toward him before–the first time her love ever held a condition. Her unsteady hands reached out to them in a limited invitation, marking this as their chance to pick sides. A frown pulled at the corners of her lips. Her shoulders threw themselves back as though she was about to snap and they'd be the ones to break her.

He'd stood on the precipice of her love in that moment. With a deep breath, he took her hand, made his choice. Even then, a dizzying awareness of what might have been lost left his stomach under assault, his heart thumping. William did the same and they continued toward the lake as their mother smiled and sang from Corinthians, "For now we see through a glass, darkly…"

A sinking dread twisted, cold and leaden, through his guts. He ignored it. Ma danced with them under the stars, spinning them in circles until they laughed and toppled onto the long grass in heaps. For a while, they sat beneath the stars and watched the moon on the lake.

Then John's stomach rumbled. He fidgeted. He opened the picnic basket and pulled out a plate of pie.

From nowhere, Ma slapped his hand. Hard. The plate flew into the grass.

John looked up at her, fingers burning, red, and aching. His bottom lip trembled.

Her wide green eyes and parted lips mirrored his own. She brought her hand to her mouth. With the other, she tugged on a lock of her long, dark curls. In a frenzy, she grabbed the picnic basket and hurled it into the water with a splash. The boys watched in silence.

A sob cut the night air like a knife in John's chest, a sharp keening sound closer to an animal's cry–he felt it as if it were his own, but it wasn't coming from his body. Ma dropped to her knees and curled in on herself.

The basket bobbed, then sank. Her dark locks fell in front of her face in a veil as she shook her head. Sobbing, she said, "William, take your brother home please."

"But –" John said.

William took his hand and obeyed the way good children obey, without question. John never forgave him, never forgave himself. Father and a neighbour pulled her body from the lake the next morning after someone had noticed a single empty plate on the shore. And so the curse had claimed Belle Toppan.

William once shared his suspicions about that night when they were much older and very drunk–how he'd seen her earlier in the kitchen grinding up flowers and plants while she baked and what he thought she planned to do to them. But John knew that was a wicked lie. He said so with a fist to William's jaw. That was the only time William ever took a hit without fighting back.

Winter 1950

Late the next night it began to snow. Sharp, polished flakes clung to the bleak fields as the wind battered the windows. And John remembered something he'd learned as a boy and forgotten: sometimes it's too late to correct a mistake, no matter how good his intentions or how desperately he wished he could go back.

William started shaking. A shake that rattled first the bed, then the house, then John. It took him a minute to recognise the violent movements as convulsions, and by the time he figured what to do, William was starting to come out of it.

Blinking up at John in a daze, William coughed hard– a syrupy red cough. When William pulled his trembling hand away from his mouth, his palm was spattered with blood. John wasn't sure if he'd bitten through his lip or if he was coughing up blood. John stared, immobilized like a fool. He had done this. This was his fault. He'd stopped, but not soon enough.

William curled up on his side, wincing, and John was fifteen again. He remembered his father writhing on the ground beside the poisoned coffee cup John had delivered after a night's beating–Father's limbs curled up in agony, lips pulled back over gnashing teeth like the dead mouse John had seen in a neighbour's barn. John's blood had shivered in his veins then, a cold pulse of horrible satisfaction. He'd wondered at the sensation, thinking, *Is this the poison in me?* When officers came, John had sat in his room at William's panicked instruction, listening through the door.

"Arsenic, it would seem. Terribly painful. You know anything about that, son?"

And William's voice, protecting him: "No, sir. My father likes his drink. Must have confused it with the sugar this morning."

All these years later, William mirrored their father's agonized face exactly. A veil seemed to flutter across his mind and John could scarcely believe the sight before him.

John's legs shook. Acid welled in his esophagus. William hadn't seen the witch spit her curse in their father's eye–John never thought it mattered, only that it made him a skeptic, but maybe William had never been a threat to John. He'd let the witch's curse damn him.

William looked at him, wiped the back of his hand across his cherry lips and chuckled. "I suppose I have had more than my full threescore and ten, haven't I, brother? Can't complain for want of a long life," he rasped.

John's mouth flapped, until: "Don't be absurd, William. You'll be fine. I'll send for the doctor." He turned to rush out, but his brother's words stopped him cold.

"Johnny, I'm afraid. God, I'm such a coward, but I am."

Something pinched hard in John's chest, a pain as sharp as glass driven between his ribs. For a moment his vision wavered and he remembered the sound of cracking ice beneath his feet.

"Johnny?"

William reached out and John sat at his bedside, clutching his brother's hand. "I'm so sorry, William," he confessed. "I —"

"Hush. You've nothing to be sorry for. You've taken good care of me. I've never been the easiest of patients. Thank you, brother. For everything." Coughing, William pushed John away. "I...I think it's time to rest now." William was so pale he disappeared into the white sheets.

When William wouldn't wake up, John stumbled toward the kitchen, his cane catching on the carpet. His steps lurched but he didn't stop. If he reached the door, he could drive to the neighbour's farm where they had a working telephone or even into town through the snowstorm, fetch Doctor Marsh, the doctor would fix William, and everything would be *fine*. William would be fine. He would stop this curse.

John halted in the kitchen.

The locked cellar door was *open*.

He frowned, touching the key in his pocket. He inched forward, peeking down the steps.

At the bottom of the stairs, something large and looming darted out of sight. John jerked back. This was no mouse. Was someone inside their home? John stared into the shadows. The gaping darkness stared at him.

Beneath the *titch-titch-scritch* of the vermin, a low groan crawled up the steps. Visceral. Pained.

John cursed. His fingers trembled as he reached into his housecoat for a match. With stiff fingers, he sparked the flame. He held his hand out to illuminate the cellar, but the light curled in on itself, collapsing under pressure until it snuffed out with a puff of smoke.

John tried again, his last match, reaching for a lamp and inching closer. He peered down the steps, ready to bolt, certain he was wasting precious time but –

"Johnny?"

The echo of William's voice from deep in the heart of the cellar so shook him that John stepped forward to meet the sound. "Brother –?"

His cane slipped from the edge of the landing, and John slipped with it.

All at once, he was tumbling, crashing.

The light smashed, but before his vision disappeared, he saw a face in the cellar he hadn't seen since he was a child peeking out from behind his Ma's apron: *the witch*.

As quickly as her haunting features flashed into his sight, she was gone. Darkness and the sickening, shivering pain of broken bones enveloped him.

The cellar door creaked closed, snuffing out the last of the light.

John stayed still, wondering if the witch watched him from the darkness, if he'd really seen her at all.

His nostrils filled with the cloying scent of musty, damp earth heavy with secrets–some he knew and some he didn't, though he protected them just the same. He'd always been his mother's son.

John thought of Ma's garden, the one she planted down here in the cellar, the bodies beneath the soil that forever tempted the vermin into their home. The sacrifices his mother made to protect their family, the soul-destroying things she'd done for the man who'd been so ready to abandon her.

Father never did discover the secrets she'd hidden from him to keep this land and family safe when he couldn't. John wondered if his poison Toppan blood seeped through the earth as he lay here now, intermingling with the bones of a hapless tax man, a pushy banker, a nosy neighbour, or someone he never met. He still remembered seeing Mr. Gilman tip over at the kitchen table while drinking the special tea his mother made. Ma had looked John in the eyes and raised a finger to her lips. "Hush, lamb. This is our secret now." She forged Mr. Gilman's signature on some documents, sent them off, and planted him in the garden.

This is God's punishment for my sins. John may have stopped there, but the thought came: The mice will feast on my flesh when I die. Perhaps even before I die.

A shiver racked his body. The chill of the cellar numbed his extremities. He assessed the damage: broken arm, likely head injury, bruised or fractured ribs, fairly minor cuts from falling upon a shelf of jars and... John coughed, noticing a thickness to the air.

As his sight adjusted, he saw the tin of arsenic he'd upended nearby, powder scattered and wafting. John shifted his broken arm and pulled a mousetrap from a mangled finger. He tried to find another match, but he'd used his last one. He fumbled with his unbroken arm until he found his cane and used it to pull himself up against the closest wall. He scouted the room blindly, still wary of what lurked there, watching from the shadows.

"William?" John called, wondering if he *had* heard his brother. How did William make it past him? Was he conscious? How did the door get unlocked?

A voice reached out to him in the black, howling emptiness.

"Little lamb?"

He dropped his cane, fingers shaking. His chest tightened. "Ma?" Blinking his burning eyes, he saw a dark silhouette. John limped deeper into the cellar.

"My little lamb, it's so cold down here," she said, her voice tinkling like bells in the night. The skittering mice silenced.

John's eyes welled with hot tears even as he coughed and choked. He stumbled further into the darkness. He'd missed her so terribly. "Ma, I did something awful... I'm so sorry. It's William—I..."

"Finding trouble again, dear brother?" William's words reached him through the darkness. "You know I can't pull you out by your bootstraps every time, don't you?"

John spun, gasping. "William?" The shadows ate his voice, consumed him.

Panting, John stumbled into the packed dirt of the wall and fell back, pain slicing through him. He pressed his hand against his chest, but his fingers were too numb to feel the gallop of his heart. He was alone here. But not alone. William found him, rescued him like always. No, that couldn't be. "You wouldn't wake up. I killed you."

John wasn't sure where the stairs were anymore. He sank to the hard earth, shaking his head, chest as tight as a vice and he'd felt this sensation before, knew it was bad. He'd gone numb to the bite of the cold, and the sparks of pain dulled. When he glanced up, a warm wave of relief seized him.

William stood over him, hale and strong. "I feel fine, Johnny. On the mend, I believe. You fixed me right up." He smiled.

"Can you ever forgive me?" John's lips formed the words, but the air didn't carry them.

"What are brothers for?"

From the shadows, Father stepped forward. His countenance was softer than John remembered. *"Water under the bridge, right, son? Surely we can all be forgiven."*

"But the curse, the poison in our blood, the witch –"

William laughed. "Haven't you figured it out? There is no curse. It's all you, brother dear."

He tried to shake his head, but his muscles wouldn't listen. John wanted to deny it, but what if it were true?

Maybe this evil had always been in him, lying in wait like the darkness in the cellar. A darkness he'd *chosen.*

Beside them, a young woman stepped from the shadows. John barely recognized her as the witch who'd terrified him as a boy. Her eyes were sad. "Ye brought this suffering on yerselves, child," she said. Though he hadn't been called a child for many years, he felt small now. "Yer brother is right. I'm no witch; there's no curse. But yer poison's all yers just the same. Ye live with yer choices and ye have to die with them too."

He knew in his veins their family *was* cursed, witch or no witch. But not the way he'd always believed. They'd brought it on themselves.

A flash caught his eye. *A mouse?* John glanced to his left, but tucked behind the boxes nearby John saw the glint came not from a rodent's teeth but from an old ice skate–one of the same ones John had worn as a boy when William pulled him from the lake. The veil that had fluttered upon his mind blew free and in a moment of brutal clarity he realized there were no mice in this cellar, and he could see stretches of wasted time with a brother who'd always protected him–even from himself.

John closed his eyes, tired and confused. A warm hand touched his cheek, melting through the numbing cold. His lashes fluttered open to meet his mother's green irises so like his own, and he thought of her bible-verse lullabies: *"...but then, face to face."*

"Come now, lamb, let's go home."

Summer Giver

... Konn Lavery

I'm not sure if this is a confession or if I am overthinking the whole thing. The prophecy. The scrolls. They were parallel to reality. Grandma's fits–or her preparation, depending on how you look at it–were clear signs.

I was adopted, as you know. A given, considering my heritage, and that the Vaans were Ukrainian. The Vaan family took me in and were quite generous. Papa–his first name was Ihor–and Mum–Maria–came here from their motherland to start a new life–the typical "sail to the New World" kind of story.

It makes one wonder why the Vaans chose this far inland. I thought at first that it was the same reason as all the others: opportunity. Coal and land. Boy, was I wrong.

At the time, the Vaans' choice to come to Alberta was a blessing. They raised me as one of their own to the point I might as well have been born in the Ukraine. I'm sure you met my grandparents, Adam, the first, and Elizabeth. Sweet, sweet Elizabeth, so keen on traditions before her health troubles.

Papa and Mum had Adam the second before I was adopted. What a strong boy. He never let the hideous animal scar on his chest stop him. I admired that about his character. He was kind, and he cared about me. I know he did. You wouldn't understand. I just wish he was more forward with how he felt earlier on. Maybe all of this could have been avoided. Maybe not.

My birth family? Well, they were neighbours to the Vaan farm. To be honest, I can't remember my biological mother and father in detail. It is like a dream—the more you think about it when you wake up, the fuzzier it becomes.

I know my birth parents were caught up in the conflict with the Canadian Militia and the North-West Rebellion, before the turn of the century. I was four when this all happened, but I know it was violent as the Canadian Militia forced their standards. They presumed we were part of the rebellion, being Métis, and despised us. I don't overthink it because I cannot change the past and I was raised as Ukrainian.

The rest of Medicine Hat was kind to us. Your father always let me see his horse whenever we were in town before the Canadian Militia arrived. They brought hell with them.

My mother and father were working on the farm when the troops showed up. I was indoors, scrubbing the floors when I heard yelling, then, the first shot. Father and Mother burst into the house as bullets soared through the windows—glass was everywhere. It didn't take long for the militia to overthrow the farm, armed with rifles and fire. Father made a distraction so mother and I could escape. I remember crying as mother held my hand as we ran, then, she too was shot, and I kept running. Eventually, I arrived at the Vaan farm. Grandma, sitting on her rocker, saw me.

After the death of my family, I went back to visit my old home. Only scorched ground remained and the burnt bones of my parents. Eventually, the farmland was taken over by the tall grasses, bluebells, and the small gophers hiding in the rubble. The remnants of the farm vanished. Such is the cycle of life when summer arrives.

You probably heard some of the rumours in town. Trust me. My family wasn't involved with the North-West Rebellion. My parents wanted a simple life, that was all.

Papa and Mum had a second child sometime after my family's death. Symon. He looked up to Adam, his older brother. As did I. Adam was going to take care of our family and make sure our parents could retire. He'd get married, as would I, and as would Symon. However, the lack of women in Alberta made competition tough for the boys. The lack of a real courtship dance wasn't the only thing. Education and proper health care were a problem. The railroad business began to grow to provide necessities and diversity to the province.

I'm rambling. I should tell you things changed when Adam proposed to move. It shocked the whole family. Mum and I were cleaning up the boiled chicken and borscht dinner at the time. We froze, waiting. You could see the betrayal and anger in Papa's eyes.

"You don't care about this family," Papa sneered.

"It isn't forever. Please," Adam said. "I would be able to build the railroad east, save some scratch."

"There is nothing but noise out there." Papa rubbed his brow. "This is why we moved here! To get away from it all." He stood up and walked away. Papa had worked all day on the farm and didn't need this from his son.

Grandma kept her head down low. She said, "Summer is coming. The gift is in you. Your grandfather would have understood. I understand."

Grandpa passed away before Symon was born. All too soon. Grandma was upset but remained a positive light in our family. We all knew she ran the farm. Papa liked to play a strong leader, but it was a mask.

Adam tried to talk to Papa again, but the talking escalated into yelling, and Papa stormed off to his room, slamming the door shut. He didn't come out for the rest of the night. Grandma stared out the window in her rocking chair, sipping a glass of vodka. Mum knitted. Symon went to bed early, because he was only a kid. Then there was Adam and me.

"Are you sure?" I asked my brother quietly as we sat in his room.

"I have to," he said. "What choice do I have here?"

"Papa can't work the farm forever."

"I know. That is why I will come back."

Adam's choice made sense. There wasn't much of a future for him in southern Alberta. Adam wanted to marry. Hell, we both did. We were of the age when our parents married and being single for so long raises suspicion amongst the townsfolk. That's why you kept pressuring me too.

"I support you," I said, taking my brother's hands, staring into his blue eyes.

He squeezed them. "Thank you," he said. "You mean a lot to me. It makes me wonder if…" he paused.

"If?" I asked.

"Nothing. I'll be leaving tomorrow." He leaned forward and gave me a kiss on the forehead. It was the first time he had done that. It seemed fitting–like a "see you soon" and not a "goodbye forever."

After giving Adam a hug goodnight, I went out to the living room to find Mum had gone to bed. Grandma remained in her chair with an empty glass of vodka. She often fell asleep in her chair.

I quietly crept up to her and slid the glass from her hand. Her eyes shot open, and she looked at me with a blank stare. I froze, not sure what to do.

"Grandma? I'm just taking your glass." I said.

"Aestatis Dator," Grandma said, not blinking.

"Sorry?"

"Summer Giver," Grandma said. "He and the devoted shall sprout from the pure."

She must be sleeping, I thought. Grandma had rambled nonsense before. It scared me, but I wrote it off as an old-person thing. I was wrong, eh?

Adam didn't say goodbye to anyone. There was no point. If he did, it would have started another fight. Papa continued his routine and didn't talk all day. Mum and I went into town, taking the carriage. My mind buzzed, wondering what Adam would do while working on the railroad. He'd meet a pretty girl and start a new life. A part of me felt left behind. I felt like I didn't belong in this world at all.

Then, reality sunk in again, and I remembered we were going to buy some potatoes. The Vaan family would simply continue life. That evening, I wrote my first letter to Adam, grateful he left me an address.

Dear Adam,

I know it is quite sudden. You just left, but I couldn't wait. The farm isn't going to be the same without you. My thoughts are clouded about the future. Mum and I went into town to buy some potatoes from Liam. He was flirtatious as always. Mum was encouraging me on the ride back to accept his advances. You know how I feel about Liam.

Grandma has been as silent as Papa, just with more vodka. They both don't have much to say. Papa is doing his best with the crops and livestock. The rain is late, and we're waiting. Symon is lost without you and clings to me now. I will do my best to fill in your shoes. I know I won't ever be you.

Enough of me. How is work? How is it out east? Tell me about all of it. I cannot wait to hear from you.

Love your sister,
Terra

Weeks went by before I heard back from Adam. Papa calmed down when he had a drink. Grandma, on the other hand, was not acting like herself. Her mood began to swing. The sweet old lady who used to bake us cheesecake tarts was no longer here. Maybe she was frustrated with the drought, like the rest of us. Her bones had ached in the past when spring arrived.

Her ramblings in a foreign language continued. I knew it wasn't Ukrainian because I heard her speak it before. This was something else. Mum and Papa didn't comment. They looked unsurprised as if they had seen this behaviour before.

In Grandma's room, I found an old book clutched in her hand as she snored. It was leather-bound with an emblem of the sun on it. I knew it wasn't the Bible. I had never seen this book before. That should have been the first sign, but I didn't think much of it. We had more important things to be concerned about–like the lack of rain.

The next day I received Adam's letter.

Dear Terra,

Things are well, thank you. I didn't get the job I wanted on the railroad. I find myself in the coal mines. The company has its hands in multiple industries and had to fill a new mining camp. You know the coal business is booming in the prairies. Life has a way of not turning out the way you expect. I feel hollow inside. The mines are dark. We start early and finish late. I never see the light.

I miss you. You understand me. At night I think I can hear your voice, calling for me to take your hand. I know it is not really you. Maybe I am losing my mind? I don't know. I think about Papa, Mum, Symon, Grandma, and you. Our family. Then I dream about the sun, lush greenery. I'm flying up, holding your hand as we rise.

I hope things look up for Papa and the farm. I won't be gone forever. Trust me. I want to return. Being in the dark mines has given me plenty of time to reflect.

This isn't meant to be an offence. Maybe we're meant to be closer than just siblings. You are adopted and not a Vaan. I haven't bedded a woman and you no man. We are pure. Good was in front of us all along. You as my wife and me as your husband. I threw it all way.

Maybe I am confused. Maybe I am lonely. I would crumple this paper out and start over, but I am out of paper and ink is low. So this is my one chance to share my words. Maybe God wishes for me to express my deepest thoughts. Forgive me, Terra. I hope things improve on the farm.

I'm not sure when I will be back, but I know I will be.

Love,
Adam

He sounded lonesome. He had regret. His confession was unsettling, but not completely crazy. He was right. I was not a Vaan. We were close, and I didn't like any of the men in town. It was a lot to take in. My main concern was Adam's feelings. He was off in a strange

land all on his own. He was also my brother.
Immediately, I wrote him back.

Dear Adam,

I am so glad to hear from you. I pray that the circumstances you find yourself in start to look up. It is upsetting to hear that the fresh start hasn't turned out to be what you were looking for. I am afraid things haven't improved much around here. The drought is worse. I suppose you left at an opportune time. Maybe you cursed the farm? I am only joking, partially. At this point, I can only pray to God that someone is listening.

I understand your feelings. I know you better than other people. I am sure the loneliness you and I are experiencing will pass. This is normal, right? Please, I treasure you in a special place in my heart. I haven't thought of us like this before, and I understand your reasoning. You can be honest with me as I have always been honest with you. We have time to think things through. Things are difficult for us both. Maybe it will all turn around, and you will meet a beautiful woman.

Love,
Terra

The last sentence weakened my heart. I wasn't sure why. Maybe it was a way of suppressing feelings I hadn't come to terms with yet. It doesn't matter now.

Weeks went by. I wondered if Adam was mad at me, but he did mention he was running out of ink and paper. His words crept up in the back of my mind numerous times throughout the spring. He didn't sound like the strong, confident, Adam that I knew.

One night, we couldn't find Grandma. She wasn't in her chair as usual. Papa and Mum went outside looking for her. They told Symon and me to wait here in case she returned.

Anxious and worried, I went back into Grandma's room to investigate. Perhaps she left a clue. I pulled open the dresser drawers, the nightstand, and the closet— nothing. I lifted the mattress. It was bare too. As I was about to leave, my foot pressed on a floorboard that levered upwards. There was a hidden compartment.

Under the floorboard was the leather-bound book with the sun emblem. There were some scrolls, a dagger, and a small bronze shrine. It had a platform for a candle and a naked man with the face of the sun and a long line running down the middle of his torso. I flipped open the book but couldn't read the words on the pages. It looked close to English, but it wasn't. I guessed it was the same language that Grandma had been speaking in.

My search ended when the front door opened. Papa and Mum had brought Grandma back. She was in her nightgown, shouting, "The Summer Giver! He has birthed! The season is near! He awaits his devoted."

"Mum! Please," Papa said.

"Silence, you disappointment!" she hissed.

I still hadn't heard back from Adam, and the weeks continued. My frustrations grew. I had no one to talk to. Symon was too young. Papa stayed quiet and only related to his liquor. Mum buried her head, pretending none of this was happening. Grandma was off her rocker, as the saying goes.

Then tragedy struck our family. Having no one to talk to, I wrote Adam again.

Dear Adam,

Papa shot himself. You leaving the farm hasn't been easy on anyone.

The drought has continued, and the animals are dying. He couldn't take it. I think he bottled up his emotions more than we realized.

Papa's death hasn't been easy on us. Mum tries to take care of the household and keep an eye on Grandma and her fits. She has gotten worse. Symon and I take care of what is left of the animals and crops.

Liam, the potato farmer, has come by too. He was kind to donate some of his harvest to us. The drought hasn't struck him as hard. Liam tried to talk to me as he always does. I couldn't. Liam mentioned I am of age and has offered his hand in marriage. It is a tempting offer. Then, I think about you. Our history. Your heartfelt letter. I sleep with it. I told Liam I wasn't ready. Please, this one letter cannot be the only one I get from you.

I beg you, write back, so I know I am not talking to a ghost.

Love,
Terra

A part of me wondered if Adam was dead. Maybe a rock crushed him in the mines. Or perhaps he met a girl and forgot about us. I didn't know what to think. I still hadn't told the family we had been exchanging letters. I feel that would have upset them. Papa had been disturbed enough, clearly. You're the only other soul that has seen these letters.

Grandma had another fit. Mum and I went out to look for her. Symon begged to join us, but I told him someone had to hold down the fort. It didn't take long to find the old lady. She was out in the middle of a field, naked, screaming at the moon.

"Grandma!" I called out.

"Adam! Where is summer?" Grandma wailed, arms outward.

"Mum! I found her!" I yelled. But Mum had gone to the other end of the farm to cover more ground.

I put my lantern down and wrapped Grandma in the blanket I brought with me. She didn't respond, just continued to stare at the moon. I knocked over something heavy with my foot. I looked down to see the small metal shrine of the sun-headed man, the one I found under the floorboards. There was a candle in its socket. The flame had toppled onto the dry ground. Quickly, I extinguished it. The last thing we needed was a fire.

Grandma turned and stared at me. The moment was too long. She smiled and said, "Of course." She reached for my cheek and stroked my face. "How could I have not seen the devoted?"

"Grandma, let's get you back inside," I said, trying to guide her back to the house.

She resisted and wailed, "Adam! Aestatis Dator!"

I wasn't sure if she missed her husband or was calling out to my brother. Then, I swear I saw Adam in the distance. He stared at us with those blue eyes. The scar. He was naked. His head glowed brightly as lightning strike. Then, only the silhouette of a man remained.

"Adam!" I called out.

"Adam!" Grandma repeated.

This is ridiculous, I thought. Realizing that I, too, was yelling into the fields, thinking I saw someone. It was just wheat crops. I forced Grandma to move with me, leaving the shrine behind. I'd come back for it tomorrow in the daylight.

Here, this is the fourth letter I wrote to Adam.

Dear Adam,

This is the third letter I have written, and I still haven't heard from you. I am greatly worried. Please, can you forgive me? A reply would be reassuring, so I know you are alive.

I think I am going crazy like Grandma. I swear I saw you in the field. Grandma was distracted, calling out to Adam. Maybe it was Grandpa or you. I do not know. But I thought I saw you. That should be a sign that I miss you. Don't you see?

Please, Adam. I need to hear from you. I haven't told anyone about our letters yet. They are between us. Come back. Mum and Symon miss you. The drought hasn't improved, and we are desperate. If it wasn't for Liam's generosity, I don't know what we would do. That stubborn Irishman, still trying to sweep me off my feet.

Love,
Terra

These letters were only supposed to be between Adam and me. They're so personal. It is like he said–life has a way of not turning out the way you expect. God, if He exists, has a strange way of strengthening faith. I would like Him to explain the sun-headed man.

The next day, I went back to find the shrine of the sun-headed man. It was gone. Grandma hadn't taken it. I know that much because we kept a close eye on her all night. Maybe it was Adam in the field after all. I don't know.

Summer was here. The rain hadn't come, and the crops weren't growing. Symon and I didn't have the knowledge or strength to save the stock. We did our best. Mum brought up the idea of selling the farm. She didn't have a plan on what to do after that, but I knew the money wouldn't last us forever. Still, it was a tempting idea.

Adam. My poor brother. I was confused. Every night I went and looked at his letter, the one about us. It tormented my mind. Maybe he was right. Maybe he made a mistake when he moved away and brought this poor luck upon us. If we had gotten married, maybe Papa wouldn't have shot himself. Maybe the drought wouldn't have happened. Even if it all had, I wouldn't have been so alone. All I have is this letter and the memory of him kissing me on the forehead.

Symon was trying, but he simply wasn't old enough. Mum had closed in on herself. She prayed to God in the same obsessive way that Grandma did.

One afternoon, Grandma was taking a nap in her rocking chair. Mum had gone into town, and Symon was working out in the fields. Curiosity struck me, and I wanted to take another look at Grandma's floorboard compartment.

Carefully, I went into her room and pulled out the planks of wood to find the familiar leather-bound book. The shrine of the sun-headed man was there. We made sure Grandma stayed in her room, but perhaps she did sneak out and get it. I don't think I'll ever have a clear answer to that.

Under the shrine, there was the dagger and the scrolls. I pulled some of the pig-skin papers out. They had crude paintings on them. There, the same naked man with a sun-head stood tall. A man and a woman lifted a baby to him as sun rays directed towards the child with a floating, flaming dagger above him, burning his chest. There were glyphs and scriptures written in the same language found in the book.

Another scroll had the sun-headed man holding the hand of a naked woman, both coming out of a baby's cracked-open chest. Flowers were in the place of the baby's guts, and water was in the place of blood. A couple of skeletons were holding the large baby up. It was quite beautiful.

Grandma groaned. I stuffed the scrolls into the compartment and placed the planks back down. That was the last time I was able to look at her storage before you arrived. This is the last letter I sent to my brother before you saved me.

Dear Adam,

I am writing my final letter to you. You haven't responded, and I can only imagine you resent me, or you have died. So, this is my goodbye letter. I felt uncomfortable after the one letter you sent me. The thought was obscure. Outlandish even. Then, the more I think about us, the more I begin to wonder if you were right. I miss you.

Things have gotten worse. Grandma makes me worried as her shouting has escalated. We've found her naked more times than clothed, dancing wildly. The larger issue is it is only Symon, Grandma, and me. Mum went to town yesterday and hasn't returned home. I'm not sure what we are going to do. Maybe she abandoned us or was kidnapped. Anything is possible. All I know is that she hasn't come back.

She brought up selling the farm. I thought it was a coward's way out. Now, I do not think so. It might be our only option.

Be well, Adam.
Terra

I don't know what happened to Mum. I was more concerned with Symon, knowing that the family responsibilities fell on me. I kept thinking about the scrolls. The sun-headed man, the baby, the two skeletons, and the lady. At the time, I wasn't sure what they were. Now, it is obvious.

That evening, after I mailed the letter, Grandma had another fit. This one was indoors. She was flailing around with a lantern, kicking the rug and chairs out of the way for more room to trot around. The ground was wet with oil. She was yammering on.

"The Summer Giver, he is on his way! Sprouted from the pure. He awaits his devoted. Summer is here!"

Symon and I tried to calm her down. She wasn't having any of it. She dropped the lantern, it crashed, and the floor lit up. I don't know how the flame grew so quickly. Grandma embraced the flame as it began to consume her flesh. She didn't scream or twitch. She raised her arms, smiling, looking up to the burning ceiling.

"Aestatis Dator!" she cried. "I bring you your devoted!"

Symon and I screamed, knowing Grandma had lost her wits. Her fate was sealed.

I attempted to guide Symon through the fire, but a beam fell and crushed him in front of me. I was trapped, coughing and wheezing from the thickening smoke. My body was scraped and scorched from the crashed timber. Alone.

Terra, my dear, came a voice. It whispered all around me. I couldn't tell where it was coming from. The crackling of the flames and the rushing wind made it impossible.

We will be united again, the voice said. It was Adam. I had to be going crazy. The heat and lack of air were melting my mind. No. I wish that were so. It was, indeed, Adam. From the flames came a bright light, moving towards me. The body of a naked man with a long, jagged scar running down his chest was below the light. The beam of light was his head, glowing too bright to see his face. The form, the scar... I knew it was Adam.

I am here for you, Adam said. He continued to move towards me, floating. The flames didn't touch him.

His hand extended outward. *Terra, my devoted.*

I reached for him as a voice shouted, "Terra!" This was a real man's voice. It was your voice, outside the flames, muffled from the crackling.

Terra!

"I see you!" you shouted.

I extended my hand, reaching for Adam. We touched–a powerful surge of energy pierced through my hand, channelling through my being. Adam flashed through my mind. Papa. Mum. Symon and Grandma. Our happy family. Then the sun. The naked man and I held hands, soaring out of a thick forest and into the cloudless sky. Vibra. It was familiar, a re-enactment of the scrolls and Adam's dream.

A firm hand snagged my shoulder and pulled me. It tore me through the flames and smoke, and out into the open air. I gasped, and sweat rolled down my face. My hair and dress were scorched. There were burn marks all over my arms.

"Terra! Who else is in there?" you said.

Reality began to take hold again as air filled my lungs. My vision adjusted to the darkness as the cool wind bit my lightly roasted body. My mind refreshed. The memory of Grandma and Symon burning, Mum missing, and Papa shooting himself were clear. The scrolls. Adam's dream. His scar. It was no animal attack; it was an intentional mark from that dagger.

The sun-headed man and his woman—no, wife... me. We sprouted from the baby. Just like the scrolls had shown. It all made sense. Adam was calling to me from beyond. His physical form was the baby. His soul was the sun-headed man, wanting to take my hand so we could be together. Male and female. Man and wife, as is the cycle of life. The skeletons—my poor family. It was a prophecy for the gift of summer. Adam was to bring it. The scrolls outlined the prophecy. Purity. Was it fulfilled? I don't think so. You intercepted it by saving me.

It was you, Liam.

"That's all I remember. I don't know what came over me," I said. "I still think of my brother, Adam." I sat across the dining table from Liam. The dim lighting made it difficult to see his expression. I wanted to know what he was thinking. It couldn't have been good. One hand was on his pistol. The other was inches from a bottle of whiskey.

"And the letters, to your… brother?" Liam asked.

"They were sent back to me, from the coal company. Adam's body was never found, just like Mum's. I can't help but wonder if the prophecy was real, and Grandma and Grampa had initiated something. A blessing turned a curse if it wasn't fulfilled. How else would you explain the drought? How else would you explain Papa shooting himself? Mum vanishing? Or how these letters survived the flames? The Summer Giver needs a pure soul to bless us with lush crops."

Liam snagged the bottle and chugged some whiskey. He slammed it back down and said, "Is that how you explain carving a knife down our baby boy's chest?"

I swallowed heavily. Liam was right. It was my rationalization, and he didn't understand because he never saw the sun-headed man. My confession wasn't enough, he'd see, when our boy is old enough to wed. When the flames come, and the Summer Giver sprouts.

The People of Open Places

... Jim Jackson

The empty space didn't expose their tryst. It concealed it as it concealed them in its vastness. The man and woman–not yet lovers, already more than friends–looked to the brake-light-lit September darkness encircling both them and the near-infinity of dry plain around the perfectly nondescript, hand-me-down sedan.

Dry air, hard with an edge of coolness, wafted through a half-rolled window. She shifted in her seat, turning to him but not looking into where she knew his eyes were. "When are you going to show me?"

She could hear his swallow over scraped-string cricket orchestras, calls of unseen birds and the steady shushing of wind through wheat.

"Show you...?"

Now she looked directly towards him. "Your drawings. Sketches." She reached for his arm in the dark and found his wrist. "What did you think I meant?"

"I barely thought anything."

She leaned back in her seat, wrapped her cotton scarf around her and looked to the land and sky distinguishable only by a slight change in deep blue. "You think I'm a slut, don't you?"

Again she heard him swallow.

"I don't," he said, a pitch higher than usual.

"You do. That's why you agreed to drive me out here. You thought you'd get laid."

Silence. Not even a swallow.

She stared out the window at the night. "You might, you know?"

"Might what?"

She turned to him. "Get laid." Back to the window. "I like sex."

"Oh yeah?"

"That's all you can think to say?"

"Um. Yeah."

"Does it make me a slut if I like sex?"

He swallowed hard. He didn't answer.

"You're a smart boy," she said into window and night. Turning back to him. "Do you want me?"

"Everyone wants you."

"I didn't ask everyone. I asked you. Do *you* want me?"

"Yeah."

Leaning toward him. "Then say it."

"I want you."

"Mm. Say it again."

"I *want* you."

She looked to the deep blue in front of her. "Turn on the headlights."

He did, lighting long grass and low scrub along the highway, rustled by wind or unseen vermin.

"See that barn?"

"No."

She leaned to him and pointed. "The dark shape out there? It's an old barn. I've got a sleeping bag and some candles there. I like to come here." She looked to him. "Now do you think I'm a slut?"

He didn't answer.

"Smart boy," she said and swung in her seat. "But show me first."

"My sketches?"

"Yep."

He reached into the back seat, brushing her scarf and the shoulder beneath it, and grabbed a dogeared sketchbook.

She leafed through pencil-scratched pages of inhuman faces–eyes just dark pits, mouths small, twisted and crabbed.

He grabbed the steering wheel. "It's. …I."

She reached for his arm, found it and fingered her scarf. "I like them."

His eyebrows shot up. "Who?"

"Your drawings. Sketches. Whatever. I like them."

"I saw something. I think. When I was a kid."

"Something?"

"Yeah. Something."

Silence.

"You don't have to tell me." She closed the book, laid a hand on it for a lingering second and opened the door, obscuring prairie night in cabin lighting. "Come on." She pulled her scarf tight around her neck and stepped out into midnight blue.

From behind a patch of low scrub, she watched the girl-man pull the boy-man towards her and press her lips to his. She felt something move at the bottom of her belly. The prairie loomed around her, she listened to its song, and she was comforted. She turned back to the girl-man and boy-man. He would be hers. She pulled the thought around herself, warmer than the rags wrapping her. He would be hers. There would be a marriage. Father had promised it.

She looked to the clean smoothness of the girl-man and back to her own rags and dust-streaked skin. She listened against the night sounds to the round sounds of the girl-man's speech and thought of her own name–her beautiful name, meaning "sweet rain"–unpronounceable by the boy-man's tongue until she bore him a baby. Father said so.

She watched the girl-man and boy-man leave the iron box and slide through dark and grass to the old man-shack.

She thought of her wedding and her bedding with the boy-man, and she thought of her hate for the girl-man for taking him. Ragged breath filled her rough burlap mask.

Smells of old and empty–so like the prairie itself–filled them as they unrolled a stashed sleeping bag and lit candles in silence. Hay dust licked at noses, and dark scratched at their candlelight halo.

Her fingers fell from her scarf to his wrist, and she forced a laugh into her voice she didn't feel. "What did you see? That you drew? What kind of something?"

He didn't look at her. "I was camping. Not far from here. I was twelve or thirteen. I was out in the bushes. I was…" His eyes shot involuntarily to his pants.

Her eyes went voluntarily. "Oh. Got it. Right–twelve or thirteen." Something in what she could see of his candlelit eyes made her stomach fall, and she reached for something that would pull them from this road. "I've done it, too, you know. It's so secluded out here in the open." She dangled the change of subject with a flirt in her voice.

He didn't bite.

"I thought it was my mother. I almost lost it trying to zip up my pants."

She leaned in, but whatever it was in his eyes made her pull back.

"It wasn't my mother."

She couldn't stop herself. "What was it?"

"I don't know. A face."

Chills shot from the back of her neck to the back of her knee. She didn't want to ask. She asked. "What kind of face?"

"It was a face that wasn't a face, in the way clouds or curtains in an unfamiliar bedroom can be a face. It was a formless shape, the size of my head, with two deep black circles where the eyes would be. But it wasn't like curtain faces. This one didn't dissolve when I tilted my head. It still looked like a face." He swallowed. "And it tilted to match me."

"Oh my god. Stop." She pulled her scarf closer.

He didn't look at her. "Do you want me to stop?"

She didn't look at him. "No. Tell me."

"It reached out a hand. It was covered in rag bandages, but it looked human. It touched me. Then it slipped its finger under its burlap rag covering its face and... licked, I guess."

Silence.

She turned to him. "Then?"

"Then I heard my mother calling. When I looked again, I didn't see the thing. Maybe I never did." He forced a laugh. "I was a kid, right?"

"Is that what you think?"

He looked to the black-blue night.

She touched his arm. "Do you think it was one of the People of Open Places?"

"The who, now?"

"The People of Open Places. Surely you've heard of them. It's a big urban legend around here. Well, *rural* legend, I guess. I heard they're what's left of an old hippie cult who moved out here to live off the land. Rumour was, they went nuts from the isolation and ate each other. Full-on Donner party stuff. No one knows for sure–all they ever found were some charred bones. Human bones."

His eyes flicked across night, looking at the darkness for details from his half-memory. For signs of humanity in those burlap-shrouded eyes.

Looking back at her. "Are you sure you still want to hang out with someone you barely know in a creepy old dilapidated barn? Someone who's seen one of those... what? People of Open Places?"

"After that story? Are you kidding?" She kissed his cheek without knowing she would. "There's no place I'd rather be."

Visions of dark eyes in burlap flicked the corners of his memory as he watched her sway peasant skirt across the open plain, grass licking her bare legs.

Alone. Candles keeping the dark safely wrapped around them. Chills more from anticipation than from prairie night.

Her scarf on his skin. A kiss. Lips and tongue and touches. Her scarf around his neck, his face pulled to hers. Sweat and dust and first-kiss sweetness fired down nerves into parts unknown but soon to be known.

"I don't want you to see me." Her breath hot.

His breath in rags. "You're beautiful. You have nothing to be ashamed of."

"I don't want you to want me for my body. Wanting my body is easy. I want you to be different. I want you to want me for my breath in your ear, for my tongue on your skin. For my body wrapped up in yours."

He tried to focus on her. "Once you take any clothes off, I can't guarantee I can keep my eyes closed."

He heard a smile in her voice as she kissed his neck. "I was hoping you'd say that." In a motion, she pulled her scarf from around his neck and tied it as a blindfold. "Now you have no choice."

He leaned back on his elbows. "Okay. Do what you're going to do."

He heard her smile deepen to a laugh. "What I'm going to do right now is go pee."

"What? Then… can I take this off?"

"If you do, then everything's off."

"Oh yeah? I like the sound of that."

"No, not my clothes, perv. All of this. We go back to the car, and you drive me home."

"It means that much to you?"

The laugh in her voice gone. "It does. Don't want me for my body. Want me for what I can do to you."

"Okay."

"Okay?"

"Okay. I'll leave the blindfold on."

She flip-flopped away into the chill of prairie darkness.

SweetRain saw the girl-man in her clean and her colour, and she felt hot purple rage. This girl-man would not be the one to take the boy-man's branch inside. Father had promised the boy-man's branch to SweetRain. It would be she who'd get marriage and bedding.

SweetRain padded behind the girl-man and saw. Saw hips sway in a way SweetRain's didn't sway, saw hair sweep in a way SweetRain's didn't sweep, saw softness in places SweetRain would never be soft.

But the girl-man didn't see her. SweetRain was one with this place and this darkness where she'd played since she could first remember Father and Brother. SweetRain's step was prairie wind, and she heard that wind whistle her to action.

The girl-man turned and squatted in the tall grass. SweetRain watched the girl-man's eyes look directly into the eye holes of her burlap. But SweetRain was prairie, and the girl-man saw nothing but prairie.

First, the tree. Dead and grey, thirty steps away. SweetRain slid through the grass, no more noticed by the girl-man than the voles and rattlesnakes who stalk these open places. She whispered the tree-prayer–blessed it for its scarcity–and broke off three branches.

Hold. Breath caught in her chest. The girl-man looked.

But nothing. The girl-man stood, tossed white into the grass and walked toward the man-shack.

SweetRain slid through the grass behind her, eyes on the girl-man, but mind on marriage and the boy-man's branch. She looked to the splintered wood in her hands, and SweetRain smiled.

The first branch SweetRain thrust into the girl-man's right kidney, paralyzing her in pain.

Then quickly in front. The second branch punctured the girl-man's left lung to stifle a screaming that hadn't yet broken the night air.

The girl-man's eyes were wet and wide, and SweetRain looked into them through burlap eyeholes. She saw pain and fear and pure, human anguish–but something else. Something light and moving.

SweetRain growled when she recognized it.

Curiosity.

Even now, with dusty wood roughed into her organs, the girl-man, like all the men SweetRain had ended, wanted to know *why*.

SweetRain had none of the girl-man's language–no way to tell her this was what Father and Brother had ordained. That she, SweetRain, would get marriage and the boy-man's branch, not this colour-clean girl-man.

In hate, SweetRain did the one thing she could to tell the girl-man why she needed to die on this plain on this night. That would show the girl-man that this boy-man belonged to SweetRain and no other.

SweetRain pulled the burlap from her face as she watched the girl-man's eyes go dark, a third branch jutting from her shattered throat.

SweetRain straightened the girl-man's body in the way Father and Brother taught to do with killed man-men. Legs extended and together, arms spread and apart. She dabbed her fingers in pooled blood from the girl-man's throat and streaked her own chest beneath her rags in sacred blood-blessing.

SweetRain smiled, knowing she shouldn't at this ritual.

She looked to the man-shack, holding in it the boy-man who would be hers. The last obstacle gone, and the blood-blessing coagulated on SweetRain's skin. Soon it would be time for Father and Brother to take the boy-man to marriage tree–pulling him from this man-world, stripping him and dressing him in sacred wild grass.

But not soon enough.

She pulled a branch from the girl-man's body, looked again to the man-shack and thought of the boy-man's branch.

Father and Brother would scold her.

She tightened her grip.

They would beat her.

Hand tighter still.

A wind picked up from far off on the flat land, and it urged her to move–to slip through the dry grass and drier ground to where her boy-man waited, unsatisfied by the girl-man.

So she obeyed mother wind and slipped into the barn. To him.

Chills licked at him, and more than once he thought he heard scurrying across the barn. No angle of his head brought him any sight from under her scarf, and he stopped trying.

"Are you back?" He called out to the dust and candlelight. "I bet you're back, and you're just watching me. Seeing if I'm going to take this thing off. Am I right?"

Neither dust nor candlelight answered him.

"Come on."

A scurry.

He laughed. "This is a test." Laughter left his voice. "Right?"

A wind picked out from the flat land outside, and it urged him to take the blindfold off.

Then he heard the door swinging open cowboy saloon style.

He angled again for a peek from under the blindfold. Nothing. But he could see her in his mind–her blouse open, her skin cool from the prairie night, her skirt trailing dust and bits of hay.

He breathed out long. "I was almost thinking you weren't coming back," he said in a half laugh.

He heard only padding footsteps moving toward him.

"Right," he said. "Sorry. Yes. No, good. I probably shouldn't talk."

Footsteps closer.

He swallowed. "That's what you're saying, right? I should be quiet? I just want to check. Because. Well. You know."

Closer.

"Okay. Good. I'll be quiet."

Footsteps stopped. Close to him.

He breathed in, about to form a word. He didn't speak.

Hands on his arms. He reached out to her, lips in a cartoon pucker, but she stopped him, gripping his wrists in night-cold fingers and holding them above his head.

Being exposed rose his blood.

One icy hand on his wrists, another grabbing the fabric of his shirt.

A yank–tearing cotton and buttons landing on ground like a half-cocked romance novel. Cool air on his chest, his own breath hot in his mouth.

Belt ripped from him, pants torn off. Naked he stood, held by her hands, in the abandoned barn chill.

He breathed hard.

No.

Her smell was wrong. It was only half her smell, half something else–grass and dust and stone.

He stopped breathing when she dumped him onto the cold, dry ground, hand still clutching his wrists.

She mounted him, guiding him inside her with chapped, calloused fingers.

Riding and writhing, he felt her warmth and her roughness–hot sandpaper against his chill-sensitized skin. She gripped him with powerful muscles.

She thrust hard on top of him, and he heard her breath deepen.

Then he heard her erupt in what sounded like bird twitter and whalesong.

"No," he breathed and pulled the scarf from his eyes.

The scarred, dirt-streaked body holding his wrists and riding him half-wore her clothes, but it wasn't her. She cocked her burlap-masked head.

"No!" he shouted, trying to move from her writhing body. Nothing. He was pinned.

"No," he half-sobbed, reaching out to hurt, to scratch, to somehow escape. His fingers found burlap and pulled.

She thrust harder as he looked into her staring eyes– as wide as his palm and black as an insect's–set in the green-tinged skin of her face. He scratched again at her tiny mouth, frozen in perpetual surprise. He grasped at the leaves crowning her head.

Nothing stopped her riding him.

And nothing stopped those staring eyes looking into him.

From the darkness behind her, two figures coalesced. The same rag clothes, same burlap mask. But big. Hulking.

He could feel the rhythmic inevitability of nature bringing him to climax despite raw, human terror.

SweetRain erupted again into twitter and whalesong as he finished inside her, and Father and Brother brought down   heavy   axes,   shattering   his   skull.

Hammers Stained Red

... Robert Bose

Iron fingers clamped my wrist, grinding bone.

"You're a killer, boy. You know it. I know it. God knows it."

"Not anymore." I tried pulling away from the old man sitting across the table. No use, of course. I was never a match for my grandfather's strength, gained through seventy years of swinging a sledgehammer.

He drew me close. "You have blood on your hands."

I stared into his bleary, yellow eyes and choked on the spicy vodka miasma enveloping him. He'd been at it since breakfast, driven to the bar on the edge of an angel's wing, but I wasn't having any of his bullshit, whether it contained a grain of truth or not.

He didn't let go. "I need you. The family needs you. The demon…"

I slumped in a hardwood chair even older than him and waved at a waitress in a tight blue dress, her familiar silhouette jutting from the bar. Sobriety was no longer an option.

"Not my demon," I said.

"It will be."

He looked pale behind flushed cheeks, flesh hanging loose. Hair whiter. Sparser. But his grip, he'd lost nothing there. Time hadn't chipped the granite underneath.

"Cancer, boy. It's got me good."

The waitress nudged my shoulder, her heat bleeding into me. I caught a whiff of Obsession.

"Hey, Angela."

"Michael." She leaned in and lowered her head with a half-twist, lips almost brushing my cheek. "Long time."

"Not long enough." I caught myself. "The town, not you."

"Around for a while?"

I avoided my grandfather's scrutiny. "No."

"Too bad, it's Corn Fest this weekend and the Class of '85 is meeting at the Palace for drinks. I… everyone would love to see you."

"Doubtful."

She gave me a playful pat. "Jesus, you're one dour fuck today."

"Unfortunately. I'll have a double whisky, neat, anything besides Crown Royal."

"You got it. How about you, Herman? Another?"

The old man hadn't said a word, hadn't slackened his grasp. He wet his lips and nodded.

"On its way." She spun to the bar, her ass holding both our gazes.

"You owe the family," he said, wrenching his attention back to me.

My mind flew back to his dirt-floored cellar, his beer-bottle throne, the tortured spirits and dirty shadows tossed from a discoloured incandescent bulb. I'd escaped that place–torn my bloodstained hands from his tools of death and ill-gotten insurance money–and hadn't looked back.

"I'm only here because Mom implied she's on death's door. She's not, is she?"

"I need you."

"You got Jim."

He sneered at my brother's name. "Worthless."

"He never did fall for your bullshit, did he? Even though he was the dependable one, the diligent one, the loyal one."

"He's weak. Soft. You know what's out there. Why it's out there."

I flinched as two glasses hit the table with a clunk. "I hope Gibson's is okay," Angela said, sliding a laminated menu my way. "Special of the day is a marble rye and mozzarella grilled-cheese with a bowl of borscht."

"Sure, why not."

She winked, snagged the menu, and flitted to the next table.

My grandfather turned my wrist to examine the tattoos crawling up my forearm: wolf and panther. "You're no different than me," he said, letting go and downing both the drinks in rapid succession, enormous nostrils flaring. "You may have forgotten what the hell is out there, boy, but it sure the hell hasn't forgotten you. Mark my words, you'll be back."

And I was.

A month to the day I walked the edge of the Taber cemetery, basting in my black suit, sun–seared grass crunching under black shitkickers. Despite the heat, the suit wrapped me like a comfortable suit of armour, the dry-cleaning chemicals almost, but not quite, overpowering the hint of wood-smoke permeating the air. You smell that, old man? Smouldering memories, clinging to both of us. Inescapable. Hope you're happy.

Knowing he wasn't, and glad for it, I pushed against the convection-oven wind to where a handful of ancient ladies encircled the open grave, tucked myself in behind my Mom's wheelchair and put a hand on her shoulder. She clasped it and squeezed. The rest of them didn't look up, though one shushed me before I even opened my mouth.

The interring was a modest affair, as old Mennonite as I'd ever seen. No flowers, no music, no eulogy. Not sombre. Almost regal. I watched my great-great Aunt Iris pick up a shovel and scoop some loose dirt onto the walnut coffin. Pushing ninety, that old bird. Her sisters, each one equally immortal, took turns, ignoring my offer to help. Ritual is ritual and this wasn't my part.

I tapped out a Marlboro, cupping it against the gusts, and lit up. We all had our rituals.

"I'm glad you came," said Mom, pulling me into a hug. "I know how busy you are up in the city. I'm thankful, and the family's thankful."

Talons of accusation raked my heart.

"No excuse," I said returning the hug, "I'm a monster. Worst son of the century."

"Now, now. I know you got your reasons. I left after high school too, you know."

"I can't stay."

"Can't or won't?"

"Where's Jim?" I asked.

Mom coughed into a handkerchief wrought with names and knots and dabbed her mouth. "Late is where he is. Called me last night, said he'd be here. He and your grandfather didn't see eye to eye, but he respects family."

Not like you. I knew she was thinking it.

"Must have been an emergency."

"I'd expect so, probably a lost lamb in the back pasture. He still has a soft spot for the scruffy things and keeps giving them names. You might want to check on him once you settle in at the Farm."

Giving lambs names. Damn. First rule of raising livestock, never name anything you plan on eating. "I'll head to the Farm right away, make sure it's quiet. I'm going home tomorrow, though."

She pulled me back down, mouth a thin, hard line, and pressed keys and a well-used hymnbook into my hands. "Don't be hasty. And call me later, okay?"

Range Road 163 hadn't changed one bit, all gravel and blowing dust, straight and boring as shit, identical in every way to every other range and township road gridding the entire south. I floated down, dodging a convoy of grain trucks until I reached Horsefly Lake, little more than an enormous irrigation slough, and took the side road to the section of farmland that'd been in our family since the late 1800s. Everyone called it the Farm, but it was more a ranch these days, dominated by open pasture and crumbling barns.

My grandfather's green International Harvester pickup sat in the driveway like it always had, worn bones piercing rusted skin. I parked, ditched my suit jacket, and clambered out into the hot wind, letting it infuse me this time, letting it strip away the soft city moss, exposing hints of stone. They called it the suicide wind, blowing day in and day out. Drove people mad. Literally. Away from the semi-sheltered cemetery, it howled, manhandling the tall bluestem grass and muffling the hum of the power line running along the ditch out front.

I'd missed it. All of it.

A dog barked, loping around the back of the house and skidding to stop. A German Shepherd, lean and scraggly. It sniffed before padding over and nuzzling my hand. Rex. He'd been little more pup when I'd left and I was frankly amazed to see him alive. Gramps had been hard on his dogs, tending to shoot first and ask questions later.

When Rex had settled down, I crouched and gave him a good scratch. "That's a good boy. Jim's taking good care of you?" At the name, he whined and cranked out a couple short barks. Not particularly helpful, but then again, I hadn't spoken dog in years. I stood and stretched, catching the wind again, shirt like a sail.

Rex and I poked around for twenty minutes, catching up on absolutely nothing, before I let myself into the old farmhouse and rummaged up a bottle of Canadian Club the old man kept for visiting dignitaries. He'd have a five-year stash in the cellar, but there was no way I was going down there today. I found a glass and drifted onto the front veranda, where I tucked myself into an oversized rocking chair. Rex joined me and instantly fell into a doze, his laboured breathing more a comfort than an irritation.

The view hadn't improved. If anything, the overgrown section of land across the road and beyond the barb wire had grown darker and denser. Tall weeds choked the hollows between scattered gooseberry bushes, stands of half-grown poplar trees, and the charred ribs of a stadium-sized turkey barn.

A tangled heart of darkness.

"What am I doing here?" I asked Rex. He had no dog wisdom to impart, asleep or otherwise, so I poured and took a sip, holding the amber liquid in my mouth until my tongue became numb. Swallowed. Repeated the process until my sight bent and the sun lurched, slewing through wisps of cloud to take a bite out of the horizon. When the glass was empty, I lit up a cigarette, hoping it would help.

It didn't.

No answers. Not even when the sunset bathed the veranda, turning my hands a deep scarlet.

Rex yawned and a low rumble gripped the air, thundering from my toes to my ears. I instinctively glanced at the Tangle, expecting the worst, but the sound emanated from the enormous mottled cat perched on the railing. The beast licked a paw, assessing me.

My grandfather called her The Countess, though she was no dainty, elegant creature. Part bobcat and twenty-five pounds of devil, backing down from nothing alive or otherwise. Another immortal, like the family matriarchs. Old. Wise. Consumed by duty and defined by ritual. The Countess rumbled again, dropped into the grass, and padded into the shadows.

Like old times.

The phone rang. I gulped back a slug of whisky, straight from the bottle, and stumbled inside. The handset was a relic. Rotary. Cracked black plastic with a yellowed center disk displaying an unreadable phone number written in blue ballpoint pen. I tried to remember if gramps was on a party line. Did party lines even still exist? Time here wasn't the same as in the city.

"Hello?"

"Hey, brother." Jim's voice hadn't changed. Never changed. At least not in my mind. Solid. Stalwart. But not hard. Never that. "Sorry I missed you at the graveside, but you know…"

"Yeah, I know. I'm half surprised you went to the service."

"Right? I showed up late, sat in the back. Escaped the first chance I got."

"That's not what Mom said."

Jim laughed. "Well, Mom is Mom. Likes her world ordered. Besides, Herman wouldn't have wanted me there."

"True. He wasn't the forgive and forget kind of guy. You wouldn't fish with him. Wouldn't hunt with him. Wouldn't kill for him. And when you didn't help burn his goddamn barn down, well, final nail in the coffin."

"I couldn't."

I let a pause stretch.

"Want me to…" Jim hit a word he couldn't say. "Want my help now?"

"I'm good. Don't worry about me, first thing tomorrow I'm out of here. His secrets died with him."

"But," he said, "they didn't. The old women know what he did. What you did. If you leave now, it'll get loose."

My skin grew clammy. "They… It can't cross the wire."

"You sure about that?"

The Tangle loomed from my vantage at the window.

His voice caught in his throat. "Whatever you decide, I love you, brother."

Rex and I put the farmyard to bed, locking gates and poking through the greying, termite-bored barns and sheds filled with incessant smoke-tinged wind and little else. Dreary. Dull. Gramps must have cleared everything out before he'd earned his release. Chores complete, I adjourned to the couch, snagging the bottle and glass from the veranda, and tried to ignore the rustling from across the road.

It could not be ignored.

A chill crept under the door and across the hardwood, seeping into my bones, fogging my breath. The demon called, taunting me. "Take up your hammers," it whispered. "Face us if you dare, coward."

I pulled a thick wool blanket over my head. Stuffed my fingers in my ears. Hummed until I fell asleep.

My childhood ritual, as potent today as it was then.

A dream took me instead, a contrast in colour. Blood. Brass. Fire. I noted each bright nail fastening the cellar steps as I shuffled one tentative foot at a time. Two bloody handprints dribbled down the wooden door. My handprints.

I stopped.

No.

I didn't have to do this. No matter what the old man expected. What the family expected. I had a choice. I'd turned away once; I'd do it again. I shouldn't be here, in this place, in this time. This wasn't my demon. Tomorrow I'd head back to the city.

The phone woke me up. I lay there, still clutching the blanket, knuckles tight, and let it ring. Over and over. Mother or brother? I had nothing to say to either of them. Wrapped in my wool womb, I didn't move. A thousand reasons to go, one to stay. It shouldn't be this difficult.

Nothing should.

It took my starving stomach to pry me off the couch, and I was relieved to find the fridge contained eggs, cheese, milk, and sausage. It was all on the edge of expiring, but edible, so I made an omelette and brewed a pot of coffee, contemplating the day.

The scales tipped with the offering I found when Rex scratched at the door to go out. A pile of bones adorned the battered welcome mat. Turkey bones. Blackened and broken. Rex stole around, careful not to disturb them while I walked to the wind-stripped veranda railing, taking in the morning glow, the morning growl. The Countess. Telling me the score.

Dammit.

The need for more coffee drew me back in. The kitchen leaked old, in every way, from the faded paisley wallpaper to the chipped laminate countertops. Warm. Comfortable. Memories of fresh bread and preserves masked by the bitter aroma of dark roast. I basked in it, downing the entire pot, before perusing my mother's hymnbook.

She'd bookmarked a page, "O God, Our Help in Ages Past," circling the second verse in light pencil and underlining the third line.

Under the shadow of your throne
your saints have dwelt secure;
sufficient is your arm alone,
and our defense is sure.

I looked out into the Tangle and remembered my grandfather teaching me to shoot. Most kids started with BB or pellet guns. Not me. Straight to .22s. Bracing on the railing and taking pot shots at anything moving in the foliage across the road, spent shell casings flying in every direction. He'd taught me to shoot. To kill.

Anything and everything. Turned my bones to stone, one death at a time, until I was hard like him. Armoured.

And I was. Wasn't I?

Wind. Always. Forever. It gnawed my nerves raw, so I fed Rex and drove back into town for lunch, ending up at the Palace, a shithole tavern in a shithole hotel. Two stoners hunched at the bar, glancing over as I came in. I joined the leaning.

"Holy shit," said the skinny one, his long crazy curls even crazier than I remembered, laugh lines pleating the corners of his eyes. "You really are back. We didn't believe the gossip."

"Andy." I nodded at him, then to the other, a heavy hitter in thick, dirty glasses. "Lee."

Lee pounded my back and shouted at the bartender for a round. "Good to see you, bud. Gonna continue the old campaign?"

"You'd better say yes, Mike, I'm tired of hearing him talk about it," said Andy, picking up his tallboy and denting it with his thumb.

"Got all the second-edition books," said Lee. "Updated my characters, the ones still alive at least. You murdered all my good ones. Repeatedly. Your bro will be in, we can put the band back together."

I laughed. I had to. That these two were clinging to the memory of my high school D&D campaign after all these years made me fuzzy.

"We never did finish that last adventure. Never killed that possessed boar in the heart of the Tangled Forest. He's still out there, waiting for us, I can feel it. All we need to do is –"

A chill swept across my arms and up my neck. I was sixteen again, squeezing through the barb wire fence across the road. I looked back, fists stained red, and watched my grandfather, snug in his veranda rocking chair, take a swig of vodka from a bottle. He caught my eye. Smiled.

"– find those magic hammers. Right, Mike?" Lee poked me. "You okay? You look like someone just stepped on your grave."

"Asshole," said Andy, punching Lee in the shoulder. "Way too soon."

"It's okay," I said. Nightmare bled into adventure. Boars and hammers and tangled forests. Five thousand tortured souls forged in demonic fire, hell-bent on avenging themselves on the family who'd sold them out for a few pieces of silver.

Unless a hero turned up. Or an even worse villain.

Lee turned in his chair, grabbing my shoulder and squeezed. "Oh shit, your granddad."

"Yeah, dude. Bites," said Andy. "Though the old goat was creepy as all hell, always taking shifts at the slaughterhouse. Always covered in blood."

The round came and we raised one to the old man because it seemed like the right thing to do.

"We missed you at Corn Fest. Cheers to Ten Years and all that jazz. Angie was pining for you. Said she saw you when you swung through town last month. Which, by the way, you suck for not showing up and saying hi. Worst friend ever. To us, and her."

"Guilty," I said. "I figured she'd be firmly in the married with children camp."

"Divorced. Remember Kevin Anderson? Total asshole."

"She knows you're back," grinned Andy. "I'd gird your loins."

Gravel crunched as a Datsun, red paint peeled orange by the elements, pulled into the driveway. Angela got out, tugged her static-clinging floral dress away from sun-smashed skin, and almost lost hold of a bulging IGA grocery bag when it caught the gale. She gave me a two-finger salute and joined me on the veranda.

I gave her a hug, returned more fiercely than I expected, and lit up a cigarette.

She ran a finger across my cheek, stole my Marlboro, and sat down on the double swing dominating the far end of the porch.

"Andy said you were staying out here, figured you might need some company. It's a lonely corner of existence." She stretched, breasts pushing against the thin dress, and grabbed one of the rods that once held a canopy over the swing. The wind had reduced the cloth to shreds, leaving nothing but ribbons of pale green cloth, wire, and a few grommets.

"You look great." More than great. Did I really want to get into this again? I tapped out another cigarette and lit it, both of us smoldering.

"Thanks, I try. I may be trapped here, but it doesn't mean I have to let it suck me dry. Hanging around for a while this time?"

"No choice."

"Yeah." She leaned back and rested a calf across her knee, showing enough thigh to spray gasoline on my flame. "I get it. But you know what," she said, rummaging around in her bag and pulling out a sloshing jug and two red Solo cups, "you had a ten-year vacation, a taste of freedom, which is more than the rest of us. Now, scoot over here. These Manhattans aren't going to drink themselves."

I sat down beside her. She poured a few fingers and pushed the cup into my hand, repeated the process, and raised hers. "Cheers to ten years."

The sun dimmed, final rays piercing the bands of low cloud and diffracting off broken bottle glass set in the stucco. The power line hummed. Crickets chirped. The Tangle shimmered, whispering in the wind.

I felt Angela shiver.

"Creepy view," she said, snuggling in and resting her head against my chest. "That the old turkey barn you used to tell me about?"

"Yeah. You can't see much of it anymore, but it was quite the thing. Housed five thousand turkeys until the fire."

"And they all died?"

"Every single one. The fire started at night, when they were all inside, asleep. Dreaming about whatever turkeys dream about. They woke up in a panic, tried desperately to escape, but there was none."

"Nightmare fuel."

"So much. I spent two summers salvaging wood out there, tracking down usable plywood sheets and two-by-fours, pulling out the nails. It got weird. Felt like the ghosts of all those dead birds were always watching. I stuck it out, though, until Gramps used the insurance money to run pigs. Not little piglets either. Monsters. Must have went around to every farm in the south looking for the biggest, meanest brutes. Said they'd make good sausage."

"That doesn't seem… likely."

"No, but he wanted them tough. Hardened. He said the Tangle wasn't fit for regular animals. He was right, there was something… lurking after dark. It pressed in on you. Full of anger. Rage. The pigs weren't strong enough. One night there was a huge racket, screaming swine, and the next morning they were gone. Vanished. Undamaged fences and those feral monsters weren't the sort anyone could steal. They never did turn up."

A snuffle and a grunt echoed from across the road. Something pushed through the weeds and scrub.

Angela took a gulp of her drink, free fingers clutching my shirt, nails digging into my side.

"Except one," I said, refilling both our cups.

She burrowed in closer.

◊

Dreams. Nightmares. The same ones I'd suffered through my childhood, suppressed by years in the city. Smoldering spars poking through thick weeds and stunted trees. Ten thousand tiny screaming lungs. Burning feral eyes, watching and waiting. Stairs leading down into darkness where a boy, who should have known better, clutched a lighter to his chest and sobbed.

A faint sigh jolted me awake in darkness. I shifted the blanket I'd wrapped us with and twisted to kiss her hair, inhale her. But she was gone. The swing was gone. The veranda was gone.

Where?

The smell of earth and fur and stale beer stained the air, and I knew. I reached up and found the dangling string.

Click.

The soft glow of the incandescent bulb cleaved the darkness of the cellar, illuminating the chair I rested upon, a massive oak throne flanked and backed by ceiling high stacks of empty beer cases. Rex breathed shallowly at my feet and The Countess purred on my lap. An enormous spiked sledgehammer, blotted and crusty, rested on a wooden table alongside a meat grinder and jars of pig's feet and turkey hearts. And more bottles. Countless bottles.

I'd turned away. Turned my back.

On him. On family.

I hated responsibility, hated the fact that sometimes, no matter how strong you were, obligation was stronger. It grasped me, claws tight. The old campaign couldn't end unless I ended it. The way I started it.

The Countess sprang away as I surged from the throne. I took a slug from a half-full bottle of vodka infused with hot peppers and strained to pick up the sledge, feeling the weight of it, the memory in it, before letting it fall with a dull thud. I didn't need it. Never did.

Stairs. Garage. Yard.

Angela's car was gone, nothing but an empty patch of overgrown gravel where she'd parked between my car and the old man's rust-covered tombstone. Regret tugged my heart, but I continued across the road, wolf and panther flanking me, supporting me as they always had. We stopped under the waxing gibbous moon. No wind. No humming power line. No rustling.

The night held its breath as we squeezed through the unforgiving barbwire fence. I let the blood flow across my hands, twin hammers stained red, as my demon trotted out of the shadows to meet me. A broken tusk. Bristly leather hide, more scars than flesh. An aura of old smoke. He regarded me with baleful, bleary yellow eyes.

"I *am* a killer," I whispered.

And stepped into the shadow, swinging.

Grasshoppers and Mountain Cats

... Rhonda Parrish

There is something about being awake before everybody else. Noises seem muffled, everything is dimly lit and you move carefully so as not to disturb those who are still sleeping. That same feeling envelops me now. Which is ridiculous. It is the middle of the afternoon and I am sitting in my idling car looking down the long, twisting driveway to the farm nestled below. But that feeling. That cautious, muffled feeling of not wanting to wake what lay dormant... that feeling persists.

I'd wondered, perhaps hopefully, whether the farm would have been diminished by time as so many other bits of my childhood have. On my way here, I'd gone to see the rocks, which had seemed immense and dangerous when I climbed on them as a child, and they'd been a fraction of the size they'd been in my memory. And the plaque giving them a name, "Old Woman's Buffalo Jump," and declaring them a National Historical Site, had somehow shrunk them even more. But not the farm.

The farm is just as I remember it.

Here, at the top of the long driveway, I am at the same level as all the crops. Wheat sweeps away in three directions and canola in the fourth. Same as always. Except, of course, they called the canola "rape" the last time I was here.

Changed the name but not the crop.

Like cutting the moldy part off a block of cheese. You can't see the rot anymore, but that doesn't mean it's not there. Doesn't mean it hasn't sunk its poisonous tendrils down deep into the core of things. What does it matter to change the name of a thing if everything else has stayed the same?

And it has.

I let my gaze travel down the length of the driveway as it descends into the hollow that contains the farm, curving slowly back and forth around three separate dugouts on the south side. To the north is a steep drop-off down to "the bog." I suppose that isn't the technical term for it, but it's what we always called it. Now, as an adult, I wonder if maybe it wasn't actually the septic field... if it was, though, surely we wouldn't have been left to play in it? But then, I think, turning my eyes toward the farmhouse and all its outbuildings, it's not as though the adults in my life had excellent judgment.

The orchard spreads out behind the farmhouse. From here the trees looked twisted and shrunken. Bereft of leaves on this late autumn afternoon. Between them and the house, I can't be sure, but I think I can almost make out the shape of the cage.

◊

Some cages you can see and some you can't. Years of support groups introduced me to the idea that addicts are sort of like lycanthropes, except that it's not the moon but their drug of choice that makes them turn. They can be perfectly normal one minute and then–snap!–as soon as their tank gets topped up to full they switch and become a different, monstrous version of themselves.

Grampa had never been like that.

Alcohol didn't make him into something he wasn't, it didn't flip a switch in him–no, it distilled him down to his essence. Concentrated him. He was always a bad man but when he was drinking he was ugly bad. Twisted bad.

The orchard out back of the farmhouse was the only one in the county–hell, it might be the only one in the province for all I knew. The farm was nestled into that little valley just so, and it created a unique climate–a micro-climate, I'd heard it called when I was all raised and grown–that would allow the fruit trees to flourish.

He had several varieties of apples back there–full-sized, not just the sour crab versions–berry bushes, and even one wizened old pear tree that never flowered but never died neither. He took care of those trees like they were his own family. Watering, pruning. Hell, he even talked to them.

My sister Alana and I had a secret hiding spot in the long, long grasses at the edge of the orchard. We'd lie there and watch him walk through the trees, talking to them and tugging on their leaves. He'd show such kindness to them they might well have been what he loved most in the world. But even so I'd watched him piss on them whenever the urge took him, so that showed just what his love was worth.

He could have sold the fruit harvest for enough to near match what the real crops made but he refused. Wouldn't even put a single fruit into the Fall Fair even though he was sure to win all his categories, what with there being no competition to speak of. He kept them all, every apple, and each year as autumn turned into winter, he'd be down in the Quonset turning them all to cider.

He worked harder at that than at any other time of year, and he wouldn't accept any help either. "You'd find some way to ruin it," he'd say. And that was on a good day. On a bad day he'd backhand you for daring to suggest it.

Most people didn't make that mistake more than once. But Alana wasn't most people. For some reason, she really wanted to help–I expect it was because she wanted Grampa to like her, but Grampa didn't like anything except his fruits. And them only because they'd make the cider that kept his tank topped up all winter long.

Well, except maybe the mountain cat. I guess he probably liked her well enough. At least until the end.

Cleopatra was beautiful when she first arrived. She was a mountain cat, all sleek lines and feline beauty. Her coat was the colour of toasted marshmallows and she paced around the cage with a grace I could recognize and appreciate even at seven. There was no mistaking it. She was gorgeous, but she'd kill you as soon as look at you. Maybe that's why Grampa liked her.

I don't know where she came from–I was young, and a girl. Nobody told me anything. But they parked her cage out back, between the house and the orchard, and I used to like to go out there and look at her. I'd lean against the giant silver propane tank, warm from the sun, and watch her pace back and forth across the front of the cage.

Some days, when it was really hot, she couldn't be bothered to move. She'd just lie back on the perch tucked into the back corner. It was painted green, so I think it was meant to look like a tree, but it didn't. It looked like plywood that had been painted green. Cleopatra seemed to enjoy it, though. She'd sprawl out across it, like a picture I once saw of her namesake splayed across a chaise. On those days, I'd sit in the shadow of the tank and just watch her. Watch the lazy way she blinked, or the rise and fall of her sides as she breathed.

I get out of the car. The hollow clunk of my closing door sounds both familiar and lonely. How many times had I come home, climbed out of the back of the family car and heard that sound in my wake? How many times had I been happy, excited about my day and the evening that lay in wait?

And how many times depressed and lonely?

The latter numbers far outweighed the former. Sad memories suffocated the happy ones.

As I walk around to the trunk, a grasshopper leaps out of my path and I smile. Those were happy memories, catching grasshoppers with my sister. They'd been much more plentiful back then, grasshoppers. Whenever Alana and I would walk through the tall grass that surrounded the yard proper and bordered the area between it and the orchard, the grasshoppers would leap and bound in front of us. I'd always hated it when they'd land on me, but I never minded touching them when it was me who cupped my hands around them. It was still skin to skin, but there was a difference in agency. In power. I was in control then, and I liked it.

Alana and I filled a one-litre Bick's jar with grasshoppers one day. There were so many they pressed against the glass, climbing over one another in a desperate attempt to break free. We tossed some blades of grass in as food, and stabbed air holes in the lid with a screwdriver. We didn't mean to be cruel.

But we forgot the jar in the hot summer sun and by the time we found it again, several days later, there was nothing to be done but to unscrew the lid and turn it upside down to dump out the bodies.

I remember looking down and seeing one grasshopper out of the multitude still alive. It lay there amongst its brethren looking pretty beaten up, but its antennas were still turning and after a moment it gathered its legs beneath it and hopped away.

I pull my stuff out of the trunk and close it with that same hollow thunk sound the door made.

Who'd have thought I would ever relate to a grasshopper?

Some days were better than others, but weekends were always bad. On weekends, I used to take my pillows and blankets and sleep in my closet. I'd bring all my stuffed animals in with me, using them to build a little sound barrier, a little cave, where I could be alone and block out the rest of the world.

I didn't let anyone in. Not even Alana. Somehow I knew that if I shared my secret hideaway with anyone it would deplete its magic. That Grampa would be able to find me there.

As it was, that only helped at night. During the day I couldn't hide away in the same way. I'd tried once, but Mom had come looking for me and forced me outside "to get some fresh air."

So those rules had been established too. At night I could hide, but during the day I endured just like everyone else.

Mom always got the worst of it, though.

Sure, Grampa would snap and snarl at me and Alana. And once, when I tripped and stumbled into the table where he was drinking, spilling his cider across the scarred wooden surface, he grabbed my arm and shook me so hard I bit my tongue and my mouth filled up with blood. But Mom was his favourite target.

Grampa would take a swipe at her for no reason other than that he felt like it. Alana and I could stay out of his way, more or less, leaping from his path before he reached us, but Mom didn't have the knack and always seemed to land right on him.

And he never called her by her name when he was drinking. He only called her "Stupid" or "Ugly" or, his favourite, "Useless."

At first Grampa bought goats and pigs to feed to Cleo. He'd bring them home alive, tied standing up in the bed of his half-ton. Rope stretched from them to each of the four corners, keeping them still and safe. Until he killed them.

Usually he did it quickly. A bullet to the head, or a knife across the throat. Usually.

One afternoon, though, he was drunk when he got out of the truck. It was there, in the way he moved his limbs, in the glassy glare of his eyes and the upturned snarl of his face. Drunk already and in a mood.

I knew someone was going to pay for it, and I didn't want for it to be me, so I backed slowly into the tall grass before he had a chance to see me. It tickled my bare legs as I moved into it, and once it fully surrounded me I lay down on my belly to better hide myself.

Still, I wanted to see what happened next, so I crawled on my belly through the grass until I was lying along the fence line, parallel to the cage. My bare feet pressed against the rough wood of a fencepost as I reached beneath my belly to remove the stone that was poking me. I rolled it away, careful not to move the grass too much. I didn't want Grampa or Cleo to spot me.

When Grampa came into view, it wasn't with a haunch thrown over his shoulder as I'd expected.

The pig was still alive. Grampa had a rope wrapped 'round its neck like a leash. Only this pig wasn't happily trotting beside him like a dog might. Its eyes were wide and rolled so far back in its head I could mostly just see white and a tiny bit of black. It was huffing and snorting and squealing. Pulling back against the rope, digging in its hooves and even trying to sit down to resist Grampa's pulling.

Grampa was a strong man, wiry but strong. Still, the pig was winning, and great furrows of earth were being dug up as it struggled against the rope.

Cleo was intrigued. I could see her nostrils working as she approached the front of the cage, and then she started pacing. Stalking the poor little pig that was being led towards her.

She was no longer sleek and beautiful, but filthy and wasted, with scabs on her body and fur falling out in patches. But she was still Death. And the pig knew it.

The pig went wild. Flailing back and forth, spitting and twisting to try and bite and the rope.

And Grampa kept pulling.

The pig wasn't moving any longer, but I could see the rope tightening around his throat. More and more.

Slaughter was just a part of living out in the country and even then, as a child, I'd seen it plenty of times. But usually it was clean, almost clinical. It made me a little sad in the moment, but it was just how things were.

But this was nothing like the dispassionate killings I'd seen before. This was cruel and–the word, one I'd learned from Sunday school but never quite had an understanding of before, came unbidden to my mind– evil.

Bile rose in my throat, and tears to my eyes.

I wanted to spring from the grass, to shout and tell him to leave the pig alone.

But I didn't.

Of course I didn't.

And the pig was squealing.

And Grampa was cursing.

And Cleo was stalking.

And then it all just stopped.

The pig fell over with a heavy thud. I might have thought it was dead but I could see its chest heaving, struggling to draw in air.

Grampa stared at it in silence.

I started at Grampa.

And then Grampa tried to drag the unconscious pig by the rope, but it wouldn't budge. So he moved around back of the animal and began to push.

It was his turn to dig his feet in, and he did.

I felt like I was holding my breath, so shallow was I breathing. I wanted the pig to be faking. Wanted him to spring up now that Grampa wasn't holding the rope any longer–spring up and bolt away.

Into the orchard.

Into freedom.

But he didn't.

Instead, a foul odour filled the air, and Grampa's cursing reached epic levels. He screamed and shouted. Stood and flailed his arms around. Then he kicked the pig in the rear end with his pointy-toed boots and wiped his hands angrily across the grass.

The unconscious pig had shit on him.

The screen door opens without a sound, and the storm door sticks in exactly the same way I remembered from so many years ago. I bump it with my hip, and it gives way.

Entering the house is like going back in time.

Except dirtier, and emptier.

It's the same grey-blue carpet in the little front entranceway. Directly in front of me are the stairs to the basement, and to the left the two steps up to the kitchen. Catching sight of movement out of the corner of my eye, I squint down into the darkness, but there's nothing there. Nothing more than mice and memories, anyway.

The kitchen floors are filthy and strewn with the remnants of God only knows how many bush parties. Miraculously the cupboard doors are all still there, though many hang open and give the kitchen the look of a hockey smile.

I look into my mother's room just off the kitchen. The plaster is broken on the walls, revealing the lathing beneath, and a giant sheet of shredded plastic dangles from the ceiling, with nothing but a handful of acoustic tiles keeping it from falling down to the ground.

The small window that looked out at the propane tank and Cleo's cage is smashed, but no breeze disturbs the wisps of curtains that hang in front of it.

I don't go look through the window. I'll see it when I see it. But first, I need to go upstairs. To my old bedroom.

I don't know what woke me. I'd been sleeping snugly in my closet nest, surrounded by the unblinking eyes of my stuffed animals, curled up like a puppy beneath my quilt. It was pulled up over my head, cocooning me in heavy darkness. It had been a hot week so I was a sweaty mess, but still I preferred my cocoon to being outside of it. Grampa had been out all night long for the past four days, drinking and making a racket outside, but deep in my blanket nest all I could hear was the sound of my own breathing.

Still, something had woken me.

There it was again. The rattle of my bedroom door's handle. Then the soft clicking sound of it opening and the pat pat of Alana's feet on the wooden floor. She was wearing footie pajamas, the kind with the plastic undersides, and I could hear them whisper against my floorboards.

I was wearing footie pajamas too, but I'd grown too big for them over the summer and Mom had cut the feet off. They were far less fun now, but still warm and snuggly. I was envious of Alana's feet being covered, and loath to break the magical barrier that protected me inside my closet, so I held my breath and hoped she wouldn't find me.

"Jess," she whispered, and I heard her move over to my empty bed. "Can I sleep with –"

Carefully, I slipped a hand out from under the blanket. My closet door was the same as my bedroom one, complete with the turning knob and the keyhole. I grasped the knob, its brass cool and smooth against my palm, and pulled. Holding it closed.

Realizing I wasn't in my bed, Alana came over to my closet and tried to turn the knob. It wouldn't budge.

"Jess, I wanna sleep with you. Grampa's…"

I could hear him, the muffled cursing and banging coming from downstairs. Alana's room was right at the top of the stairs, while mine was down the hallway. It was no wonder she'd heard him first. He was definitely growing louder, though, winding himself up to a great explosion.

But I couldn't let her in. Letting her in would break the spell.

I didn't answer her, just held the door closed with all of my seven-year-old strength.

She stopped in mid-sentence and I felt her grip on the knob loosen. There was a sound of movement, but not of retreat. She was still right outside the door. Breathing. Waiting.

A long moment passed in which Grampa stomped and snorted downstairs and then I felt Alana release the doorknob completely and listened as her plastic-bottomed feet shushed out the door.

I knew where she was going. I hoped she could stay out of Grampa's way for long enough to get there.

The closet is smaller than I remembered. More pathetic. There is nothing left to remind me of the sanctuary it had been for young me on so many nights. The magic, if there had been any magic, was long gone.

Now there is a piece of what looks like a broken bong and a discarded condom curled up on the corner beside it.

A yowling scream–like one of Cleo's roars–echoes through the house and I freeze in my tracks. Holding my breath. Waiting for it to repeat.

It doesn't.

Must have been the wind tearing through a crack in the windows. The cracks in the walls.

I recall how still the curtains were in Mom's old room, hanging in front of the broken window, but I dismiss the image with a shake of my head. Sudden bursts of wind happen on the prairies. Even in the hollows.

Still, a new sense of urgency stirs me out of nostalgia and into action.

The fumes sting my eyes as I douse it–all of it–with gasoline. I cover the floor and splash up the walls. And then I make a trail out the room, following the path Alana would have taken that night.

Out of the bedroom, down the hall. I pause at the top of the stairs near the bathroom and, more poignantly, Alana's bedroom. Steeling myself, I look inside.

There is no furniture left in it, nothing but the random detritus left behind after teenage parties, but I could still tell it had been a young child's room–even a stranger would be able to. The bottom half of the walls were painted pastel green and the top half a soft pink. Carousel horses pranced around the border between the two.

I remembered Mom, heavy with her pregnancy, painting those horses and talking about how it was going to be once the new baby came. She'd been so proud of the space she'd made for her. So full of dreams and plans. And for that time, that brief window when Mom had been expecting Alana, Grampa had behaved himself. He'd still been an old grump, but he'd been sober, and that made a difference.

Then, when Alana was only a few weeks old, the news had come about Dad. He'd been working for an oil company somewhere… somewhere not here… and there had been an accident. He wouldn't be coming home.

Grampa had started drinking again and if Mom had ever had the ability to stay out of his path she lost it once his son died. She just didn't have it in her to leap anymore.

I splash the gasoline into Alana's room for good measure and then continue to stream it in the hall. As I turn to go down the stairs, I feel eyes on me and look anxiously over my shoulder. There's no one there.

Nothing there. But I still feel as though I'm being watched, as though I'm being stalked.

The first jerry can runs out as I return to the main level so I toss it into the kitchen, open the second and turn right into the dining room. After giving it a good, long soaking, I head for the front door.

Something warm stirs against the back of my knees. Just the wind, I tell myself again, even though it feels more like breath than wind.

I move quickly out the door, out of the shadows of the house and onto the porch. Here, the fading sunlight and the warmth give me the courage to look back at the stream of gasoline that leads out of the shadows to my feet. Make me calm enough to explain away the tracks in the gasoline that look like they belong to a big cat, to tell myself it's just the result of an uneven floor, shadows and a powerful imagination.

I splash the entire porch in a quick moment, and then it's time for me to step off the stairs and into the sea of grass that surrounds the house.

Back in the day, the area immediately surrounding the house had been kept mowed, but now it has been left to grow wild and the grass is almost as high as my waist. I don't want to step into it. As much as I want to get away from the open doorway and I know there is nothing to fear there–the most dangerous thing it could be hiding is a skunk–I still hesitate. Torn between two unknowns.

The sun has moved in the sky and the gasoline fumes are making me light-headed by the time I am ready to take those last few steps.

◊

The pig shitting on Grampa was the final straw, the ultimate insult. When I saw it happen I knew what was going to come next. I wish I'd been able to stop it. I wish anyone had been able to stop it. But that pig's fate was sealed.

He was still breathing when Grampa finally maneuvered him between the two doors that led into Cleo's enclosure. Cleo had jumped up onto her perch as he'd approached–even she knew to keep away from Grampa when she could–but she slowly unfurled herself and slunk down to investigate just as Grampa gave the pig one last shove into her enclosure and closed the first door behind himself. He was barely out the second before Cleo attacked.

The pig, who had been barely aware, hardly conscious, made one horrible scream, a heart-wrenching squeal like metal on metal that would forever be branded on my brain, and then he fell silent.

Cleo tore him apart. It was eerily quiet. There was only the sound of her huffing and tearing and chewing.

Blood and gore spattered the cage and dripped from her muzzle while Grampa leaned against the propane tank with his arms crossed over his chest and smiled with smug satisfaction.

When I finally step off the front porch and into the long grass it feels like jumping off a dock and into a lake. Going from one world to the other.

In that first world, the porch world, I am a full-grown adult, with a family of my own and a successful legal practice. In that world I live in the city, where I've just finally buried my grandfather, who'd wasted away in a nursing home for a decade–too ornery to die until he was old and decrepit–and accepted this farm, which I haven't seen in twenty years, as my inheritance. A farm perhaps best left alone to vandals, the elements and the past. A symbol of agrarian decay.

Standing in the grass, though, I am suddenly a child again. Terrified. Hiding in the closet and counting on magic to protect me. I am helpless and alone.

After the day with the pig, Grampa fed Cleo less and less. I heard him and Mom argue about it once. Mom said if he couldn't take care of the animal he ought to give it to someone who could. And he said what the fuck did she know anyway? She was just a useless cunt who should learn to take better care of her whelps and keep her nose out of his business.

Each step across the front of the house feels like a battle, but I win them, one after another, and continue to trail the gasoline behind me. When I reach the corner, I don't hesitate–in fact, I speed up and smile wryly as a grasshopper jumps out of my path.

And then there it is. The cage.

The only person who should have been out that night was Grampa. Mom couldn't have possibly known that I wouldn't let Alana into my closet. Couldn't possibly have known about her secret hiding spot out in the orchard. Only Alana and I knew about that, and I'd never tell…

Only the bars remain, like some rusted-out skeleton. The floor, Cleo's perch, even the doors are all missing.

Still, as I start to walk towards it, I feel as I had when I was little, eyeing it warily, uncertain how much to trust that the bars would keep me safe from Cleo. Would keep Cleo on the other side. My heart thuds in my chest and the hand holding the slowly emptying gas can starts to tremble.

I pause, grabbing the handle of the jerry can with both hands, breathing slow like the parade of psychiatrists I'd seen over my lifetime had taught me.

In.

Two. Three. Four. Five. Six.

Hold.

Out.

Two. Three. Four. Five. Six.

In.

◊

There were no trials. Cleo was hunted and shot, and mom... well, she wasn't fit, they said. Sent her to a hospital and me to live with her sister.

And, of course, she hadn't meant for that to happen to Alana. When she'd opened the doors to Cleo's cage– Cleo who was starved and half-crazy herself by then–it was Grampa she'd thought would be out wandering in the darkness.

I heard the abbreviated scream, even from within my closet, and I knew what it was.

I couldn't possibly have known, and yet I did.

And that scream shattered the spell that had protected me, safe in the embrace of my stuffed animals and my quilt.

Shattered my life.

I bolted from the closet and tumbled down the stairs.

But mom wouldn't let me out to see.

Wouldn't let me out to try and save her.

Mom died in the psychiatric facility three years later. "Released herself," she called it in her final letter to me.

I was eleven.

◊

The propane tank is gone, but the concrete slab it had been mounted on is still there. I stand on it and listen to the frogs and the crickets sing.

The house, on my left, is empty and gaping. The windows broken, the walls stripped of all their paint and weathered to grey. The orchard to my right is overgrown, the boughs that I can see broken and twisted.

It is autumn. There ought to be fruit, but there isn't. They are as barren as the rest of the homestead.

Soon it will be night and I want to be gone by then. To watch the flames from the top of the driveway before I turn my back and leave forever. The fire won't burn the bars, of course, but that is hardly the point, is it?

I come up to the cage. Walk through the empty doorways like walking into the gaping maw of some giant beast.

I rush to empty the rest of the gas can, though I lie to myself and say it is because night is falling and not because I am still terrified of this place.

Is that the faint odour of cat piss? Even now? Even beneath the sharp scent of the gasoline?

Surely not.

Surely.

Not.

I turn and flee the cage and sprint through the long grass, back to the front of the house.

I pull his lighter from my pocket. Grampa's. A Zippo, with a sprawling tiger across its front.

It isn't a cougar, true enough, but the fact he would have a big cat on his lighter. The one he carried in his shirt pocket against his heart until the very day he died. The fact that he would make that choice after everything that had happened…

I flip the lid open.

Thumb the wheel.

Throw it.

The gasoline catches with a womph that knocks the air from my lungs.

They say cougars attack from behind. Knocking their victims to the ground and driving the air from their –

The fire zips toward the house.

Dry. Old. Empty. It is engulfed in a matter of moments.

I want to see the cage, to watch the flames dance between the bars, but don't dare. The long grass is burning too.

I could hear Mom's voice screaming as she had that night: "Not you too! I won't lose you too!"

The flames roar, like a big cat, but I turn my back on them.

In my car, when I reverse to turn around and go up the drive, I pause to watch the place burn, but it is difficult to see clearly through all the bug smears–mostly grasshoppers–on my windshield.

I turn on the washer fluid and the wipers. Wait until they've done their work and I can see what I need to see.

And then I drive away.

Grass Gods

... Elizabeth Whitton

They whispered to her.

When the wind blew. When it didn't. When the sun rose high above, freckling her pale skin. When it sank into the earth in the evening, swollen and red.

During the night...

They told her things. Curious things. Baleful things.

Hungry things...

Today, as the grass whistled and moaned, a scent in the dust-filled air made their quiet voices keen.

Beware...

He's coming.

So she sat in the willow chair on her porch and watched the long rutted road carving its way from a black point on the horizon to her front door. While she waited, she slid her thumb down fresh pea pods from her garden. Sweet green pearls dropped with soft plunks into the huge stainless steel bowl on her lap, making it ring.

The bowl was half full when he unlatched the gate.

The hard planes of his face sheened with perspiration, and damp hair hung over his forehead, black as a raven's wing. He'd slung his leather jacket over his arm, and held a phone in his hand. Though tall and ruggedly built, he moved with an easy roll of his hips that made his steps more a prowl than a stride. He could easily subdue her, but that wasn't what made goosebumps prickle her arms.

Power swirled around him like an invisible cloak.

"Hey there," he said, white, square teeth flashing against bronze skin. "My truck broke down a ways from here." He held up the phone as he came to stop a few feet from her porch steps. "Couldn't get any cell reception to call a tow truck. Now my battery is dead."

She nodded "Coverage can be bad out here–it depends on your provider." She carefully set her bowl of shelled peas on the porch floor and rose to her feet. "I'm Abbey."

"Haden. Haden Acheron," he replied, shoving his phone into his blue jeans pocket. He leaned down and picked up a rusted hacksaw that lurked in the grass by his boots. "Could hurt someone," he muttered as he examined its russet-stained teeth.

"Where are you from?" Abbey asked, staying out of handshaking range. She wrapped thin arms around her chest though the late afternoon sweltered.

He glanced up, and her breath caught at the intensity of his stare.

"Calgary." He nodded toward the far off mountains etching the horizon. "I'm a landman for an oil and gas company. Just out and about, checking some easements when my damn truck broke down."

Silence fell, heavy and expectant. Only the lazy drone of a bee disturbed the hush holding sway over them. The beginnings of a cool breeze, sharp with the tang of rain, teased a strand of pale hair loose from her bun. She pushed it behind her ear.

His eyelids half-lowered in a lazy way and he smiled.

"Storm's coming," she said, glancing at the thunderheads roiling toward them from the south, their towering cloud tops pristine white, the sky behind them black with a sickly green cast. She had watched them build all afternoon.

"Sure is."

"Well, I guess you better come inside if you want to use my phone." She opened the screen door for him. When he walked past her and through the shadowed doorway, she shivered.

He still carried the hacksaw.

Haden sat at her ancient yellow Formica table as he surveyed the country-sized kitchen. He'd left the hacksaw leaning at a precarious angle against the back door. The slightest touch would send it crashing to the floor.

"Nice place." But he seemed to search for flaws. Water stains on the ceiling. Cracks in the wall. Holes in the wide baseboards.

His gaze rested on the faceless doll made of dried grass lying on a side table with an offering of purple salvia beside it.

Haden turned to her. "Just you out here?"

"No. My husband will be back any time," Abbey lied, as she handed him her phone and a glass of lemonade.

Drops of condensation on the tumbler wobbled as her hand shook.

His gaze slid to her bare left ring finger when he took the glass.

Then he bent his head and started texting.. The sleeve of his chambray shirt moved up revealing the jagged beginnings of a tattoo. She tensed as he scrolled through her phone.

A few minutes later, he frowned. "Must be quite a storm coming our way. There's a tornado warning out for the area. My company can't send anyone to pick me up until it's over," he said as he set her phone on the table beside his lemonade. "I may have to impose upon your hospitality for a while."

Her hands clenched within the folds of her denim skirt.

"Of course," she said.

He stared out the gingham-framed window and took in the bald prairie beyond her weathered barn. "I notice you keep your fields fallow—more than just one season by the look of it. There's good earth out here. If you don't want to grow crops yourself, why not rent it out?"

"I like it wild," she said. "Besides, there isn't much natural prairie left. Soon little rabbits and gophers will have nowhere to hide."

Haden gave her an indulgent smile as he leaned back in his chair and clasped his knee with linked hands. He observed her as she tidied up vegetable leavings on her red-stained chopping board, his eyes not moving, as if watching TV.

"Why a carving knife?" he asked.

Abbey jerked at the sound of his voice. "Pardon?"

"Why use a carving knife to chop vegetables?"

"Oh...' She glanced at the knife in her hand. "It's the sharpest knife in the house." She set it in the kitchen sink.

His gaze intensified as he searched her face as if trying to scry her secrets. "If you don't mind me asking, is Abbey your full name? Or is it short for something?"

"It's just Abbey," she said, her mouth suddenly dry.

The ramshackle windmill by the barn creaked as it began turning in a gust of wind that rippled waves in the wild rye and timothy. A flash of light followed by the rumble of thunder shook the windowpanes. Then the wind picked up, raising dust and sending dandelion seed heads helicoptering into the sky. Pea-sized hail pelted the ground.

"The storm's arrived," she murmured as she leaned to look out of the window. She turned to him. "Would you like some borscht?" She pointed to the chipped enamel pot full of bubbling soup on the stove. "I made it today with beets and fresh dill from my garden."

He beamed. "I haven't had a homemade meal in a long time. I'd love some."

The hail stopped, replaced by fat raindrops that made splatter marks in the thirsty soil. Rain lashed the kitchen window as she ladled ruby soup into blue china bowls and set them on the table.

Haden devoured the soup. "This is delicious," he said, his spoon scraping against the bowl. He wiped his mouth with a napkin, leaving a red smear on the linen. "But you didn't use beef stock. Are you a vegetarian?"

"Vegan." She took his bowl to refill it. "I don't eat meat or animal products of any kind, not even cheese."

"I couldn't do it myself," he said, shaking his head. "I like my steaks dripping blood." She set a second bowl of red in front of him.

The walls of the house creaked as a rogue wind gust battered it. There was a crash of thunder and the kitchen light flickered twice before it died, leaving the kitchen in gloom.

Abbey lit candles. Their wavering flames battled the murk with limited success—the storm had turned early evening to night. They finished their soup by candlelight, and when Abbey started washing the dishes, Haden checked her phone again.

"Shit," he said under his breath.

"What is it?" asked Abbey, her arms elbow deep in bubbly water, her hands patting for the carving knife.

"The bridge on the secondary road out of here just washed out." He stood up and walked toward the sink. She twisted around to face him, her hands dripping. He stopped a couple of inches too close, making her back up until the cracked linoleum countertop dug into her back.

She looked up into black fringed eyes. Grey. They were grey. The colour of ice over a dark winter lake. His lips held a cruel twist when not curved into a smile. Close up, she could see how his muscles pulled at his shirt; how his large hands could fit around her neck and –

"Look, I know this is incredibly inconvenient, but do you think I could stay the night? My company will pay you prime hotel rates, and I'll be fine sleeping on your couch."

Abbey blinked before pasting on a brilliant smile. "How can I say no?"

"Great!" He grinned. She sagged when he left to explore the living room, her phone still in his hand.

She pulled the knife from the sink and wiped it dry, then slipped it, handle down, into the deep well of her skirt pocket.

Stealing toward the back door, she avoided the places where the floor joists creaked. She reached for the hacksaw propped against the door.

A small shadow flashed past the hallway door and skimmed up the stairs. Followed by another. And another.

The hacksaw slid between her outstretched fingers and fell to the floor with a clatter.

"Look what I found," Haden appeared in the kitchen, holding a bottle of merlot from her stash in the living room closet. "My company will pay for this too, if you—hey, are you okay?" His forehead creased beneath a fall of black hair. "You're as pale as a ghost."

"I'm fine," she murmured. "Sure, let's drink it in the living room."

As she searched the cupboard for wine glasses, his gaze burned like acid into her back.

"Don't you get lonely out here?" Haden cradled his glass of merlot, his eyes bright in the gloom of the shabby living room, the rest of his face swathed in shadow. The last flickering candle created a shrinking island of light in a black lake without shores.

"I like being alone," she replied, her glass untouched on the battered coffee table. Gone was the pretense of wayward husbands returning home.

"But you're young. You should be out in the world, having fun with friends, going to movies and clubs. Instead, you live in a run-down old house in the middle of nowhere, twenty miles away from your nearest neighbor."

"I prefer my own company most of the time," she answered.

He said nothing, forcing her to fill the silence.

"People always seem to... want something from me." She stared into the blackness surrounding them. "I'm safer here."

He tilted his head. "Are you?"

Abbey swallowed hard as she reached for her wine.

"I think so," she murmured.

Abbey drank half the wine in the glass before setting it down. His eyes flashed silver when she wiped a drop of wine from the corner of her mouth with a long, slim finger.

"So what about you," she said. "Are you lonely?"

He regarded her for a long minute. Something passed across his features, softening them. Disappointment? Regret? Grief? She couldn't tell.

"I do get lonely, actually. I've travelled the world, been to places few people have seen, witnessed strange and even miraculous things. Yet sometimes, I wish I led a different life."

"You could, you know." Abbey leaned forward, her soft lips parted, her eyes suddenly alive. "Lead a different life. You could choose another path right now. Just like that!" She snapped her fingers.

She laid her hand on his, her touch feather-light. "I believe it with all my heart."

Haden stilled in his chair.

The last remnants of the storm left with one distant rumble of thunder. The walls ceased creaking. A ray of moonlight slanted through the living room window, piercing the darkness with cold, blue light.

Haden blinked as if waking from a spell. He shook his head, and the planes of his face hardened as he pulled his hand away from her. "No, I've chosen my course. I know what I want, and it's worth any sacrifice to obtain it."

Abbey's expression turned solemn. "I'm sorry to hear that."

He laughed, the shadowed moonlight turning his smile feral. "I'm not the one you need to pity."

A rustling sound, then the stomping of little feet running above made him start. "What the hell…?" He jumped up and stared at the ceiling, then shot an accusatory look at Abbey. "Who's upstairs?"

"No one," she shrugged. "I'm used to weird sounds coming from the attic. It's probably mice or squirrels. It's impossible to keep them out."

"Mice?" Haden settled in his chair, incredulous. "If I were you, I'd get a cat."

"No," she shook her head. "I don't like them."

"Why not?"

"They're cruel," she replied. "They play with their food before they eat it."

"Yes." Haden picked up his wine glass, thick eyebrows tenting above gleaming eyes. "They do, don't they."

But Abbey didn't pay attention, because the lines of the tattoo on his wrist began glowing. She rose to her feet.

"It's getting late. I'll grab some blankets for you."

She lay under her duvet, wearing her thin cotton nightshirt, the carving knife clenched in her left hand at her side.

Waiting…

The full moon rising outside her window washed the room with a blue glow, its silver reflection a distorted orb in her dresser mirror.

The door remained silent as he pushed it open. He stood in the entrance, wearing only his jeans and boots, his broad chest alive with runes glowing red like cracked earth over lava. His eyes, no longer dark, glittered icy white, and in his left hand gleamed the hacksaw.

He walked to her bed, his steps soundless on the floor, and the bed didn't creak when he sat beside her, though the mattress sunk under his weight. He set the hacksaw against her night table.

"Pretty…" He lifted a strand of her wheat-blonde hair. "I didn't expect you to be pretty. Or kind. You really are a gentle soul."

He dropped the curl and traced a finger down her cheek to her neck, leaving a trail of heat in its wake. She stiffened when he clasped his hand around her pale throat.

"So why don't you give me the knife you took from the kitchen. We both know you won't use it on me."

She gripped the knife handle so hard its metal handle bruised bone. Then she relaxed, pulled it from under the duvet, and handed it to him.

"Thank you, Abbey." He took the knife with his free hand, while keeping his other firm around her neck.

"You know, I don't believe Abbey is your full name," he said as he eased his grip. "The funny thing is, I find people always leave clues about their true names."

She shuddered as his fingers followed her collarbone and slipped under the lace edge of her nightshirt. "I guess deep down, people just want to be known for who they really are." He lifted the fabric, revealing a tiny tattoo of a blade of grass where her collarbone met her shoulder.

"Grass," he murmured to himself. "A name meaning grass…"

He smiled.

"Abelene."

The word vibrated in the air.

Invisible cords wrapped around her and pulled tight, making her gasp. She couldn't move, couldn't raise a finger, could barely breathe. She lay rigid on the bed, only able to move her eyes in wild jerks.

"Don't struggle," he said as he rested the sharp edge of the blade against her cheek. "It won't help. I'm a wizard. A caster of spells woven with words, and now I know your true name."

Haden stroked her lower lip with his thumb. "So soft…" he murmured. Abbey's eyes widened, her chest rising and falling with each ragged breath she took.

He sighed and sat back, holding the knife on his lap. "I search the world for people like you–vessels of power. Send out seeking spells. Cast bones." He shook his head with grudging admiration. "But you hid so well I'm still astounded that I found you at all. And what a find! You thrum with energy; it ripples the air around you." His eyes darkened with desire. "It sings to me."

Haden touched her nose with a playful tap of the blade. "You don't even realize it, do you? What you are. What you could've become. All you know is that dark things seek you out–want to possess you. No wonder you prefer the isolation of desolate places."

He tilted his head, his features now alien and inhumane. "It's nothing personal, Abbey. But I need your power, and there is only one way to harvest it."

He ran the knife down her cheek, but she couldn't flinch at the sting as a ribbon of tiny red drops welled against her white skin. He stood and slid the blooded knife under his belt at his side, then picked up the hacksaw.

"Let's go for a walk."

◇

Stars glinted overhead, chips of ice flung across the black cloudless night. Abbey stumbled, rocks and thorns digging into her feet and making them bleed, the parched ground already hard again. Haden ignored her plight. He hummed cheerfully as she followed him, jerking with each step like a pull toy on a string.

"I saw your altar in the kitchen. Which deity do you worship?" he asked, as if making pleasant conversation to pass the time.

"The grass gods." The words came, yanked out in gasps.

"Ah, the lords of little things," Haden nodded. He turned to her, his forehead furrowed. "Is that why you thought you were safe out here? Did you think they could protect you?"

His questions tugged for answers like a hook in a fish's mouth.

"Yes." The word tore from her throat in a ragged whisper.

He laughed. "They're the gods of mice and beetles and worms that burrow into the earth; the tenders of thistle and hay, nothing more. The grass gods can't save you, Abbey."

They came to a bluff of young poplar trees growing on the edge of a coulee. The trickle of the creek that cut into the prairie below them mingled with the trill of a nearby cricket.

"Let's stop here," he said, and she dropped to the ground. She lay on her side, unmoving, her eyes wide and focused on the hacksaw.

"What?" Haden followed her gaze and lifted the hacksaw. "Oh. You think I'm going to use this on you." He started to laugh. "No, little dove. I'm going to use it to cut firewood."

She sagged.

Haden pulled the carving knife from his belt. "This is what I'm going to kill you with.

"I'm going to build a bonfire on that knoll.". He pointed with his hacksaw to the highest point on the prairie for miles. "And when the moon reaches its zenith, I'll slash your throat and soak the ground with your blood. Then I'll throw your body onto the flames and burn you to ash. For once its vessel is gone, your power must seek a new one."

A cold smile lit his face. "Me."

He shrugged. "It's either that or eat you. But that would require a lot of chewing, and I'm still full from supper." He laughed again.

The grass rustled as he began to saw a tree with preternatural speed.

The flames of the bonfire shot up high, releasing angry orange sparks into the night like clouds of glowing insects. Wood broke with ominous snaps as it burned white-hot, warming Abbey's face, though she lay immobile a good twenty feet away.

Haden drew a wide circle around the inferno with the carving knife, chanting as he dragged its point through the dust. Power began swirling in the air, thick as the smoke billowing from the burning greenwood. As he chanted, the wind picked up, whipping the flames into a tornado of iridescent colors, twisting with fierce, hungry beauty. He raised his arms to the moon overhead, no longer silver but malevolent yellow. His chants reverberated in the earth, in the air, in her.

Then he lowered his arms, his runes glowing so bright that his body and face lapsed into shadow. His white glass eyes settled on Abbey. He walked toward her, his hair shifting in jagged pieces over wide cheekbones.

The carving knife in his hand...

Seed heads and narrow streamers of dried grass rubbed against each other, trembling in the wind. Waves undulated in a moving carpet of timothy, fescue, and wild rye.

"We come," they whispered.

"We come."

The grasses parted and she saw them. Little shadows stepping into the firelight, twisted foxtails for hair, shiny black beetle casings for eyes, runes in bird dung painted on their cheeks. Twigs pierced their noses.

Barely a child's knee high, they wore skirts of dried sage that rustled as they emerged from the prairie night and surrounded the wizard and his burning pyre.

He sneered at the small creatures, but the scoff slipped from his face as they kept coming, countless as the blades of grass whispering in the black prairie night.

The wizard spun around in a slow circle, the carving knife held out at his side. His power contracted into him in a rush, releasing Abbey from his spell. She gasped, drawing in a full breath for the first time since he had bound her.

He reached back with an open palm to the fire. Flames arched toward him in a fiery stream, spinning into a small orange sun above his hand.

The grass gods drew in closer.

"Igniti!" he cried and hurled the ball of flame at them.

The orb bounced from one little god to another, lighting up their hair and burning the twigs in their noses. The smell of scorched sweet grass filled the air. Silent screams tore into Abbey's mind as the gods ran in frantic circles, patting their heads with grass fingers that caught fire.

Haden laughed. "Burn, little lords," he shouted. "Burn!"

Abbey climbed to her knees.

"Immadesco," she whispered.

The flames died on their bodies, leaving only wisps of smoke tendrilling above their charred heads. The wizard whipped around, mouth twisted in rage, realization blooming in his face.

"You're a caster!" he hissed.

She laid her palm flat on the hard prairie earth.

"Radices vinctum," she answered.

Roots from nearby wolf willow bushes snaked along the ground and wrapped around his legs, pulling them tight. Haden twisted as they coiled up his chest, battling to keep his left hand free. He dropped the carving knife and sliced his hand through the air. The roots fell to the ground in writhing pieces.

Abbey stood, runes glowing under her thin nightgown, pale hair whipping about her face, eyes glittering ice white.

"You forget, caster," Haden snarled as he raised his hands. "That I know your true name."

He mouth twisted into a malevolent smile. "Abe –"

And they swarmed him in a wave of golden grass.

They crawled up his legs, up his chest and onto his head, then over each other, until he resembled a giant haystack. He lurched under the weight of the growing mound before toppling to the earth.

Abbey staggered toward the grass-entombed wizard, bending to pick up the discarded carving knife on her way. She reached through the writhing mass of dried grass and hay until she found hair. She pulled up and the little gods fell from his face and neck. Haden's eyes rolled, his mouth stuffed full of thistles, blood dripping down his chin as he made garbled sounds, trying to cast a spell.

"The grass gods may be small," she said, as she yanked his head back, exposing his throat. "But there are many of them."

She bowed her head. "We thank you for presenting yourself as a sacrifice."

He jerked his neck back and forth, the whites of his eyes showing as Abbey leaned down until her lips brushed his ear.

"It's nothing personal, Haden," she whispered. "But we need your power, and there is only one way to harvest it."

Abbey straightened

"Utinam digna sit hostia sanguinis deis meis!" she cried, raising the knife to the ancient stars and the baleful moon.

May this blood offering please my gods.

She drew the blade against his throat with an economical slash. An arterial gush of blood sprayed the little gods, turning their upturned faces red. They slipped from the wizard as he writhed and kicked his legs, his hands clamped around his neck. But the blood continued to pump out between his fingers, soaking the earth beneath him.

The gods gathered around him in a tight circle, countless bodies deep.

Watching...

Abbey dropped the knife and collapsed onto the ground in a lump. Groaning, she examined her battered feet by the blazing firelight. She had plucked out several thorns by the time Haden's last gurgles ceased and his body stilled

One of the gods touched the red-brown mud with a tiny burnt finger. The group turned to Abbey, singed skirts rustling, beetle eyes shining. She lowered her bloody feet and straightened as they gathered around her, sewing her tight into a circle of grass.

Then joyful voices rang through her mind as they began jumping up and down like excited puppies.

"Okay, okay," she muttered. "Give me a second." She stood and limped to where Haden had left the hacksaw.

True, she was vegan, she mused as she carried it back to Haden's corpse.

But the grass gods liked meat.

Copyrights

More

For more, go to <u>ThePrairieSoul.com/press</u>
Prairie Soul Press

Made in the USA
Columbia, SC
25 November 2020